“They’re my boys, too, Lara.”

“We’ll get them back tonight, right? And then this will all be over and everything will go back to the way it was before.”

The way it was before. Her and the boys in one place and him living a fake life somewhere far away, deep undercover. “Sure.”

She gave him a smile that warmed his heart. “We make a good team, don’t we?” There was something in her eyes…

He knew without a doubt that danger lay ahead for both of them. They couldn’t pretend that if they gave into temptation, it would lead somewhere this time.

“What we have here…” He paused. “Don’t over-estimate it, okay?” He was warning her off, even though he wanted nothing more than to kiss her. “To get those boys back, you would have teamed up with the devil.”

“Maybe I did.”

DANA MARTON

THE SPY WHO SAVED CHRISTMAS

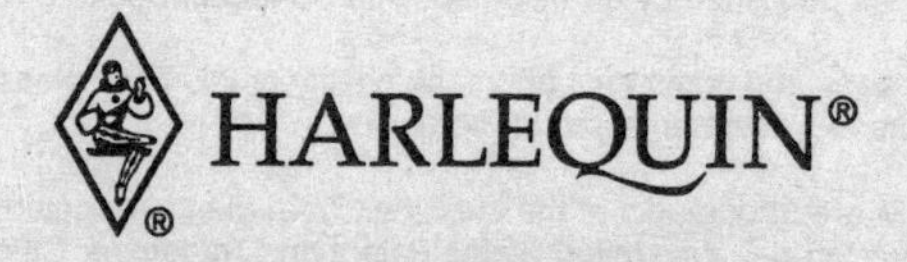

TORONTO • NEW YORK • LONDON
AMSTERDAM • PARIS • SYDNEY • HAMBURG
STOCKHOLM • ATHENS • TOKYO • MILAN • MADRID
PRAGUE • WARSAW • BUDAPEST • AUCKLAND

With many thanks to Allison Lyons.

Recycling programs for this product may not exist in your area.

ISBN-13: 978-0-373-69502-7

THE SPY WHO SAVED CHRISTMAS

This edition published by arrangement with Harlequin Books S.A.

For questions and comments about the quality of this book please contact us at Customer_eCare@Harlequin.ca.

www.eHarlequin.com

Printed in U.S.A.

ABOUT THE AUTHOR

Dana Marton is the author of more than a dozen fast-paced, action-adventure romantic suspense novels and a winner of the Daphne du Maurier Award of Excellence. She loves writing books of international intrigue, filled with dangerous plots that try her tough-as-nails heroes and the special women they fall in love with. Her books have been published in seven languages in eleven countries around the world. When not writing or reading, she loves to browse antiques shops and enjoys working in her sizable flower garden, where she searches for "bad" bugs with the skills of a superspy and vanquishes them with the agility of a commando soldier. Every day in her garden is a thriller. To find more information on her books, please visit www.danamarton.com. She loves to hear from her readers and can be reached via e-mail at DanaMarton@DanaMarton.com.

Books by Dana Marton

HARLEQUIN INTRIGUE

806—SHADOW SOLDIER
821—SECRET SOLDIER
859—THE SHEIK'S SAFETY
875—CAMOUFLAGE HEART
902—ROGUE SOLDIER
917—PROTECTIVE MEASURES
933—BRIDAL OP
962—UNDERCOVER SHEIK
985—SECRET CONTRACT*
991—IRONCLAD COVER*
1007—MY BODYGUARD*
1013—INTIMATE DETAILS*
1039—SHEIK SEDUCTION
1055—72 HOURS
1085—SHEIK PROTECTOR
1105—TALL, DARK AND LETHAL
1121—DESERT ICE DADDY
1136—SAVED BY THE MONARCH†
1142—ROYAL PROTOCOL†
1179—THE SOCIALITE AND THE BODYGUARD
1206—STRANDED WITH THE PRINCE†
1212—ROYAL CAPTIVE†
1235—THE SPY WHO SAVED CHRISTMAS

*Mission: Redemption
†Defending the Crown

CAST OF CHARACTERS

Reid Graham—A lone-wolf commando soldier, on loan from the SDDU to the FBI. Reid became the best by making sure he had nothing to lose. When his past rises up and suddenly there's more at stake than he could have ever imagined, it might just be his undoing.

Lara Jordan—When a domestic terrorist cell kidnaps her twin sons, she has no one to turn to but Reid, a man whose secret life she's only beginning to understand. He's clear about one thing—when the mission is over, he'll leave again. The smartest thing she can do is make sure she *doesn't* fall in love with him.

Kenny Briggs—Moving up in the ranks of the cell, Kenny wants to take down the government as badly as he wants to avenge his father's death. And he has the full support of his family.

Joey Briggs—The middle brother, Joey, is fully on board with their plans, and his past experience with demolitions should come in handy.

Jimmy Sparks—Is he simply another member of the group, or is he something more?

Cade Palmer—Retired SDDU soldier, Cade is at the right place at the right time to help Reid.

Colonel Wilson—Head of the Special Designation Defense Unit.

SDDU—Special Designation Defense Unit, a top-secret military team established to fight terrorism. Its existence is known by only a select few. Members are recruited from the best of the best.

Chapter One

His hands were stained and rough-skinned. Large. They were the hands that testosterone hath made, she would think later, when she could think. His grip was all male and possessive. His fingers dug into the pale skin at her hips.

Something in her responded to him. *Everything* in her responded to him.

"You have that wild streak of your grandmother's, Lara Jordan." Her mother had poured her disapproval on Lara every chance she got. "Mark my words, girls like you come to a bad end," she used to say, then would add with a disgusted glare, "every time."

Lara had fought that parental prejudice all her life, only to realize now that her mother had been right. At the urging of the man who was kissing all common sense from her, she lay back on the wood-topped table—flour dust be damned—and let him situate himself between her legs.

She was twenty-two, alone in life for the first time, and she was about to lose her virginity to the most dangerous man she'd ever set eyes on. And she couldn't claim for a moment that he'd seduced her. She was the one who'd strolled over to his bakery next door with a trumped up excuse, after hours.

"Here we are, the butcher and the baker," she said just so there'd be something in the air beyond their panting.

He licked a fiery trail down her neck and stopped to press his hot lips against her racing pulse. "If a candlestick maker tries to interrupt, I won't be held responsible."

They groaned together at the lame play on the nursery rhyme.

She didn't know any candlestick makers, but she thought she might have found the candlestick.

Oh, my.

Her skirt came up. Her panties slipped away. His mouth scorched her nipples through the thin fabric of her bra. She ran her fingers over the corded muscles of his back. He was almost a full head taller than she and built like a brick oven. She was built like, well, like a butcher, but she felt feminine next to him, desirable in his hot gaze from the beginning.

When she'd decided to take over and run the butcher shop she'd inherited from her uncle, she'd considered that she might be getting in over her head. She had no idea how deep. But this was the life she wanted—adventure, challenge, and not the staid, average existence her mother had lived, where every move was dictated by rules and more rules. She was going to be wild and free.

The man between her legs lifted his head, his dark gaze burning into hers. He said one word only, "Mine."

"Yes," she whispered as he pushed inside her with incredible restraint.

They'd known each other for a week.

Two years later...

THE DAY HAD BEEN GOING to hell in a handbasket even before his past decided to rise up and spit into his face. Undercover agent Reid Graham watched with mixed emotions as Lara Jordan walked in on the arm of a corporate stiff whose suit cost more than his monthly government salary.

Of all the restaurants in all the world, and she walks into this one. Tonight of all nights.

Lust and anger hit him in the gut in about equal doses. Lust, because the memory of their one night two years before was still his number-one favorite fantasy. Anger because a single word from her could blow his cover and jeopardize an operation in which he'd invested years' worth of sweat and blood. One wrong word could easily get the both of them killed. And not just them. He glanced around the crowded dining room, frowning at the people, who could go from innocent bystanders to victims in the blink of an eye.

Dammit.

"So you're definitely not a cop." Jen, the coldly beautiful blonde sitting across the table from him, played with her food.

"Hell no, darlin'." He wasn't lying. Technically. "I'm a friend of a friend." He gave her an easy, relaxed smile. "Hey, I've been where you are now. Gets easier. Believe me."

Soft Christmas music danced through the air, the room filled with the scent of pine. The walls were decorated with about two dozen Christmas wreaths, each labeled, showcasing contest winners from local schools.

He pretended to be scanning the holiday decorations while he stole another glance at Lara. She was laughing up at her guy, her face lit like a Christmas tree. Her hair was shorter than two years ago, her impossible curls swinging around her jawline, leaving her creamy neck out there for everyone to see.

Something deep inside his gut twisted.

"I want out." Jen put down her fork. "I want to disappear. I'm not handing the CD over until I get that guarantee. And I want money."

"Let me work on that." Tonight, he was Dave Marshall, a shady figure who operated in the gray area between the two worlds of right and wrong, with connections in each. "Got anything to prove that you're serious about this?"

She glanced around, then pulled a black cell phone from her purse, slid it across the table. "It's Kenny's backup phone. I pretended that mine broke and borrowed it for today."

He palmed the phone and stuck it into his jeans

pocket. "I'll have it back to you by morning. How you doin', darling?"

She glanced down, her hand going to her still flat belly. "He doesn't know. I'm not gonna tell him either. He took up with that bitch. The jerk thinks he can keep us both." She gave a disgusted snort. Then a sigh. "My sister knows." She moved her hand back onto the table.

For a second her shirt gaped, and he could see the small firearm she carried. A good reminder that she was more than a frightened pregnant woman who was trying to leave her two-timing terrorist boyfriend. She wasn't exactly as pure as the driven snow, although she was playing the damsel in distress to the hilt.

"I only got involved in the whole mess because of him." She put a touch of vulnerability in her voice. "You can get me out by this time tomorrow, right? Before they notice the CD is missing. Dr. Julie said you can do anything." She flashed him a smile that promised carnal benefits as his success fee.

Dr. Julie Lantos—emergency care provider for injured criminals who preferred to avoid hospitals, and an informant on the side—had referred him to Jen. Dr. Julie had an illegal drug habit that her shady patients supported, and the FBI agent she passed information to overlooked.

Reid leaned back in his chair and smiled right back at Jen. She was hot and she knew it. She was used to running with men who could get her exactly what she wanted. If becoming her new best friend—or more—was what he had to do to get information on the sleeper cell he was investigating, then so be it. It wouldn't be the worst sacrifice he'd ever had to make for his job.

She straightened her back. Her D-cups jutted out even farther, the glittering tank top she wore under the open shirt stretching enough to show a clear outline of her nipples.

Maybe if Lara hadn't been in the room, seven tables down by the window, he would have been more impressed. But she was there, and she threw him off his game. So instead of suggesting to Jen that they go someplace private to talk some more, he asked, "How about dessert?" And told himself that he was only stalling because if he stood up he might draw Lara's attention.

When Jen's foot ran up his leg under the table, he sighed with weariness and pretended it was pleasure. If it came down to it, if it was the only way to get her to talk, he would sleep with her. The terrorist group he was investigating was in the endgame of something big. They were ready to make their move, and he still didn't have any idea what was going down or where.

Even if hitting the sack with Jen meant ending his career, or that she couldn't be prosecuted because he would have messed up her case, he would do it to save lives. That was his priority. And he was determined to keep his eyes on the prize. He'd been in the business too long to toe any line without asking questions, to obey any rules that went against his better judgment. Too many lives had been lost. He'd *taken* too many lives. Something inside him desperately needed to make up for that. He would do whatever he had to do this time. There were no limits.

If only Lara would get up now and walk away.

Instead, she looked up and straight at him, blinked once, hard, before her eyes grew wide with shock, her face going pale.

"Hey, you know what?" He pushed to standing. "Forget dessert. Let's go someplace more private."

Jen picked up her purse and stood at once. She was game.

He left a couple of twenties on the table, enough to cover their dinner, tip and then some. Jen's smile widened as she put on her coat. Whatever anticapitalist principles the cell embraced, she sure didn't look like she was the enemy of money.

Lara was standing, too, saying something to her date, her eyes still on Reid. She looked softer, a little curvier than he'd remembered. She moved forward, her elegant black silk dress clinging to a body that had nothing to do with planklike photo models and everything to do with filling a man's hands in the most perfect way.

He shrugged into his jacket, took Jen's arm and pulled her behind him toward the door.

Lara's step faltered. Then she gathered herself and kept coming toward him.

He figured the distance to his car. They weren't going to make it. The gig would be up the second Lara called his real name, Reid instead of Dave. They were at the door. Through it. He scanned the parking lot that took up one full block.

The lights of the city blocked out the stars in the sky. The buzz of New York filled the air, the sound of millions of cars and people. To the locals, it was a beloved symphony. The tourists usually found it energizing and exciting. The constant buzz annoyed the hell out of him. How was a guy supposed to hear his enemies coming?

He pulled his keys from his pocket. "Hey, why don't you get in the car? I better pop into the bathroom before we leave. I'll be back out in a minute."

Jen pulled her coat together as she reached for the keys.

Then several things happened at the same time.

Lara came out the door—sooner than he'd expected. Could be she had run. She wrapped her arms around herself as the wind hit her. "Reid? What are you—"

Her voice was lost in tires squealing as a dark SUV whipped up to the sidewalk and two masked men, one in the passenger seat and one in back, opened fire.

Reid dove for Lara, vaguely aware of Jen hitting the ground like a pro behind him. He gathered Lara against his body and rolled for cover behind a massive sign that advertised the restaurant.

A bullet penetrated the sign just an inch from his face, a good reminder that flimsy barricades, car doors and such, only stopped bullets in the movies. But at least the cover kept the shooters from being able to take exact aim.

When the shots had quieted for a second, he stuck his head out. The SUV was backing up to get closer to them.

He shoved to his feet and yanked Lara up, dragging her behind him, lunging for cover behind the closest car, then the next and the next as bullets pinged around them. Then he was by his own car at last, and the next second they were inside, and then he was driving, getting the hell out of there, having momentary advantage in going forward while their pursuers had to drive in reverse.

The last thing he saw before he shot out onto the busy boulevard was the dark SUV turning around to follow, and Jen's lifeless body in a pool of blood, illuminated by the light over the restaurant's entrance. An image straight from the scene-ending shot of an old-fashioned thriller.

Except this was real life, *dammit.* And he had just lost his most promising asset in a top-priority case. His teeth ground together as he stepped on the gas, weaving in and out of traffic.

"Reid?" Lara's voice sounded uncharacteristically weak.

She was pressed into the seat as far as she could be from him, looking like she was seeing a ghost. Which she was, in a way. As far as she knew, he'd died a little over two years ago, the night he'd lost all control with her at the bakery.

"I don't understand—"

"Hang on."

He couldn't afford to be distracted now. He scanned the rearview mirror and swore under his breath.

He should have shot back at the bastards. If he'd got them, Jen would still be alive, his narrow doorway to the cell still open. If he'd injured them, the FBI could have interrogated them. If he'd shot them dead, fingerprints could have still been collected. Clues. Links to something.

Instead, he'd lost Jen and gained absolutely nothing.

Gained Lara's life, a small voice said inside. And he found that as badly as he'd messed up tonight's operation, he couldn't work up any serious rage. Which didn't mean that plenty of anger didn't simmer below the surface.

Still dazed, Lara was straightening in her seat, gathering herself. "But you died in the fire."

He turned down the next street, took another turn, then another, going in the opposite direction he had been before. He watched his rearview mirror for the dark SUV, but couldn't see it. "I don't have time to explain."

Why in hell did she have to show up in his life now? Why did she have to show up at all? *Ever.*

She put her seat belt on with hands that were unsteady but not shaky. She had good hands. Working hands. Strong. She was no shrinking violet. Even now, minutes after escaping mortal danger, she was pulling herself together. Lara Jordan was one tough chick. He'd always liked that about her. As much as he ever let himself truly like anything about anyone.

For the most part, he was big on keeping his distance.

Of course, there'd been a time or two when he'd

slipped. Like their one night together. He hadn't made that mistake since. If sex was offered and the time was right, he took it. But he was always up front about what he was and wasn't willing to give. There was no loss of control, no passionate coming together against all reason with...with a virgin who had stars in her eyes, for heaven's sake!

His teeth ground together. Between the shoot-out he was leaving behind and the memories that were quickly surfacing, sending heat straight to his groin, he was getting more morose by the minute.

"Where are we going?" Her voice was nearly back to normal.

"Someplace safe," he bit out, even as his mind worked a mile a minute trying to think of such a place. He could only come up with one. *Oh, hell.*

"Who were those people?"

He turned left at the next light. "Not now." They'd finally made it to Brooklyn. He pulled up a familiar street, slowed in front of an unassuming row house, hit the garage opener, pulled in, closed the door behind them immediately.

She peered through the darkness. "Is this where you live?"

"Mostly." And he'd never, *ever* brought anyone here before, friend or foe. He would have to move now. Dammit.

He grabbed her hand and dragged her across the seat, out on his side as he left the car. He froze in place for a second when she stumbled against him. "I'm not going to turn on any lights. Just follow me." Stepping away from her, he punched in the security code then opened the door that led inside.

She tripped a couple of times, not knowing the terrain, but he couldn't slow for her. He wanted them in the den with its reinforced walls and his arsenal of weapons close by.

"Here." He stopped by the hall closet and handed her his Kevlar vest. "Put this on."

She obeyed without a word.

Then they were all the way in. He pushed her down onto the couch and went to stand by the window. The street was quiet. Not that he allowed himself to relax. He'd been in the game far too long to make that mistake.

"What happened back at the restaurant?" she asked.

And he closed his eyes for a second against the voice he hadn't forgotten in the past two years, the voice that had said, "*Yes, oh yes, Reid, please,*" as she'd come apart in his arms on the bread table in his bakery, another undercover job that had turned into a disaster.

The muscles clenched low in his belly.

"What are you involved in?" She folded her arms in front of her awkwardly, the vest, a little big on her, limiting range of movement. Moonlight glinted off her full lips, off the dimple in her right cheek.

He turned fully toward the window, getting her out of his peripheral vision. She was nothing to him. A hot memory from his past. There was no reason why the sight of her on his couch, in his house, should bother him at all. She had no power over him.

She could have had. He'd realized that early on. Which was why he'd made the decision to never go back. He took her power away by reducing her to a memory, a sexual fantasy. He could take her out when he wanted to, and he could put her away.

"Are you involved in something bad?" Her voice held a new twinge of nerves.

He gave a short bark of a laugh. "What do you think?"

Silence stretched between them.

"I'd like to go." Her dress rustled as she stood.

He turned back to her, which was a mistake. The black silk clinging to her thighs did nothing for his focus. He fought the impulse that was pushing him closer to her. "You can't."

"Reid—"

"They saw me leave with you. It won't take long for them to ask a waiter who you were with in the restaurant. Then they'll go and ask your boyfriend about you."

He swore under his breath. Somehow, his cover had been blown. The shooters would connect Lara to him. Her boyfriend was probably being worked over right now. Chances were good the poor bastard wouldn't live to see the morning.

"I need to go home."

"By now they know where you live. It's not safe." He gentled his voice with effort. "You can stay with me." Until he could get the authorities to take custody of her and figure out long-term protection. Which, he hoped, could be arranged in the next couple of hours. He had to get back out there and find Jen's CD before anyone else did.

That CD was his holy grail. The cell's leader had trusted Kenny with its safekeeping. There had to be something on the damned CD that would provide a clue on the planned attack.

"It's all over now," he told Lara. For her anyway. For him, there was still a long way to go. "I'll make sure you're protected."

Instead of thanking him for the offered protection, all hell broke loose as she flew at him.

"Why isn't it safe to go home?" She grabbed him by the shoulders and shook him, looking ready to tackle him if necessary.

She'd always been a strong woman—had gone to school on a sports scholarship, been sidelined by a knee injury, had taken over her uncle's butcher shop when the guy had retired.

He captured her wrists, tried to pull her against him to subdue her. Easier said than done. She was almost six feet of wriggling fury.

"They'll go to your house," he tried to talk sense into her.

And then she started fighting in earnest, this time to get away from him, her eyes on the door. "Let me go." Her arms were wheeling like windmill paddles.

"Lara?" He caught an elbow in the chin, and swore

under his breath. All he needed was to get his arms around her, but she wouldn't cooperate.

"I have to get to Zak and Nate." She kicked him, backward, viciously in the shin.

"Whoever they are, they'll have to take care of themselves." How many men did she have in her life?

"Are you crazy?" She screamed the three short words, elbowing him in the chest this time, doing her best to cause permanent damage. "They're babies."

Babies.

The guy at the restaurant was probably her husband. A cold sensation spread through his chest. Which was beyond insane. He barely knew her. She was a mistake he'd made two years ago. A momentary loss of control that should have never happened. What did he care if she'd gotten married since then?

He almost had her where he wanted her when, suddenly, she dropped her whole weight in some self-defense trick, and took him to the floor with her. But he was too quick to be shaken off so easily. He was on top of her the next second, his hands restraining both wrists above her head as he used his weight to hold her down in a pose that brought back some old memories and woke up his body.

She strained against him, which didn't help any. "If anything happens to Zak and Nate, I'll kill you. Do you hear me?"

He was aware of the curve of her hips under him, her long legs entwined with his. More memories rose and flooded him. His limbs went paralyzed. For a second, he couldn't move anything from the neck down. And there wasn't much activity from the neck up either.

For a heartbeat, nothing existed but searing need.

Dammit. He'd thought he was done with this.

Then his body came alive with a bolt of pain as she kicked him where it hurt the most and shoved him off her. She dove for the door.

He couldn't breathe. He rose anyway and lunged, caught her by the knees and brought her down harder than he'd intended—he didn't exactly have full control. "Sorry."

"Sorry isn't enough." She kicked at him one more time, missing his face by an inch.

He compartmentalized the pain and somehow got her pinned under him again, more carefully this time, taking no chances. "Stop for a second, would you?"

"Get off me." She did her best to head-butt him. Her eyes burned with hate and desperation as she wriggled, hissing and threatening murder.

Hot memories aside, one thing was becoming crystal clear: this Lara wasn't the Lara he still dreamed about sometimes, still fantasized about, the Lara who'd so sweetly surrendered to him.

Where the hell was the timidly curious virgin he remembered?

Chapter Two

She had *grieved* for him.

Lara fought, blind with fear and anger. She'd grieved for him when his bakery had burned, with him inside, hours after she'd left him that night. And she'd grieved again when she'd found out that she was pregnant, grieved for her babies who would have to grow up without a father.

But he hadn't been dead. He'd been alive; he just hadn't cared enough to tell her, too busy taking knockout blondes to dinner. He was involved in some nasty stuff, probably organized crime or drug dealing or something.

God, what an idiot she'd been.

"I go to your grave almost every Sunday, you jerk." She tried to shove him. Might as well shove a brick wall.

Reid looked taken aback. "I have a grave?"

"The town buried you when no relatives came forward. They paid for the lot. There was a collection to pay for the coffin. I paid for the service. From my insurance money." Even with him standing in front of her, she could still feel the lingering grief. Obviously, her mind was having trouble catching up with reality.

"I'm sorry."

She tried to heave him off. "If you say you're sorry one more time, I swear I'll kill you."

He managed to restrain her at last, the bloody bastard. "You're a lot more violent than I remembered."

She stilled. Mostly because there was little else she could do. And also because he was right. She was acting completely out of character.

She'd threatened murder twice in the last ten minutes. This wasn't the kind of person she was. It wasn't the kind of motherly example she would want to set for her boys.

"Must be rubbing off from you," she shot back, as confusion, pain and humiliation hit her in quick succession. She tried to shift under his familiar weight, looking for a way out. "Please let me go." For her babies, she would beg. "I won't say anything to anyone. I'll forget I ever saw you again. You can be dead to me again. I want you to be dead to me."

Some dark emotion passed across his face, but it was gone before she could identify it. He waited a beat, measuring her up, then pushing away. "Okay. Cease fire."

She nodded because he was stronger than her and she had no other choice. He'd always been tough and rough, had bad boy written all over him, the very thing that had drawn her to him in the first place. He was the hottest-looking guy she'd ever known, opening up shop right next to hers the week after she had. She was a goner the first time she'd laid eyes on him—six feet four inches of muscle and attitude.

She swallowed hard, pushing those memories away as she sat up. "Are you sure those men will track me down?"

"They'll follow any lead they think might lead to me. Your kids are at your house?"

"Yes." She buried her face in her hands. Her heart beat out of control. "With a babysitter." God, she'd known that going on a date as far away as New York City was a huge mistake. But Allen had asked, not for the first time, and everyone she knew was on her case, telling her that she needed to get a life and move on. So she'd said yes.

The guilt was going to kill her. If worry didn't kill her first. She rose to her feet and glanced at the door, weighing her chances of getting by Reid.

He was dialing his phone. "Hey. I'm fine. I'm heading out. I'll call you back when I'm on the road. One thing right now. I need protection in Hopeville, P.A." He gave her address.

Strange that he would remember. He hadn't bothered coming back to tell her that he was okay. She couldn't have been that important to him.

"Whoever you have closest. Local cops, fine. Outside surveillance, not to go in unless needed. Anyone approaching but me should be considered armed and dangerous. There are kids inside," he added, then hung up and walked to a wall panel that opened to reveal a frightening cache of weapons. He tossed boxes of ammunition and guns into his bag, along with hand grenades and other things she didn't recognize.

And the guns weren't the scariest by far. The measured way he moved, his cold method as he assessed each weapon before selecting it spoke of a man who wore danger and violence like a second skin. How could he have hidden it so well two years ago when it was obvious now?

She inched toward the door. She really, really needed to leave.

"Where do you think you're going?" he asked without looking her way, keeping up with his preparations.

He could have been the hero of some action movie. *Or the villain.* Two years ago, with his tattoos, the fact that he rode a bike, with those bedroom eyes of his that awakened her body for the first time to the fact that she was a woman, he was the most dangerous man she'd ever met. Just talking to him had always been a thrill. But he was so much more than she'd ever known.

"Please let me leave." To think that despite her stunned reaction at the sight of him in the restaurant, she'd been so incredibly happy to see him. Sitting there, alive, he was the answer to all her prayers. She used to have dreams like that. His coming back, telling her it was all a big mistake. The two of them making a real family. His promising that he would love her forever, would never leave her again.

And now her fondest dreams were turning into a nightmare in front of her eyes. She pressed her jaw together for a second until the pain passed. "Please let me go home," she entreated once she could breathe.

He barely looked up. "I can get you there faster than anyone else. Guaranteed."

He was going to take her? "No offense, but I'm not sure I want you anywhere near my babies." She thought of the gunfight at the restaurant. The way he'd left his date there, lying in a pool of blood. Okay, she was sure she didn't want him anywhere near Zak and Nate. And she kind of wished she'd never told him about the twins. She'd been still too shaken up. Hadn't been in her right mind. Hadn't been able to think.

He closed the panel. "I'm one of the good guys."

She kind of figured that from the phone conversation, and would have been lying if she said that wasn't a great relief. But... "Good guy and dangerous aren't mutually exclusive," she pointed out. "Whatever you're involved in, I want no part of it."

"Too late."

Was that regret in his voice?

He took the few steps necessary to reach her, and she had to look up at him. He was a good couple of inches taller and almost twice as wide in the shoulders—and she wasn't a small woman.

He hesitated for a second, then huffed some air out through narrowed lips. "I was working undercover tonight."

A couple of things clicked into place. Her mind raced. "And back in Hopeville when we met?"

He tossed her a coat, then once she'd put it on,

grabbed her by the wrist, heading out to the garage. "Yes."

Of course. He'd been new to town. But then again, she'd been new, too. They had bonded over being outsiders who were trying to get their small side-by-side shops going, trying to fit in.

"Is Reid Graham your real name?"

"Yes. I was hoping to find a way into the cell through an old army acquaintance who knew me back then. He'd gone the wrong way after he quit the army. He has a cousin on the fringes of the cell. My record was doctored to make it look like I quit, too, shortly after him. I ran into him 'accidentally' and was trying to get into his confidence. Anyway, I had to use my real name."

"Who was the blonde at the restaurant?"

"An asset. She had information I needed."

A disposable asset, apparently. Obviously, his business involved using people and casting them aside if necessary. Then she thought of something else, and her throat constricted.

"Was seducing me part of your cover?"

"You came to me." His voice was low, tightly controlled. "But regardless—" He paused while he let his car quietly roll out of the garage. He was scanning their surroundings. "What I allowed to happen…plain bad judgment on my part."

Tears burned the back of her eyes as they reached the street and he stepped on the gas. She looked away from him, blinking rapidly, staring out the side window at the houses that zoomed by.

"I have a situation here." He was talking on his phone again. "Personal. I need a safe house somewhere near Hopeville, P.A." He listened. "Not much. I have the tag numbers of the SUV the shooters drove." He rattled that off, then looked at her. "What's your husband's name?"

Husband? Oh, Allen. "Allen Birmingham."

"Anybody by the name of Allen Birmingham at the restaurant?" His face darkened as he listened to the response. "I figured," he said before ending the call.

She gripped the seat belt. "What? What happened to Allen?"

"The cops talked to him when they showed up. They asked him to wait in the manager's office because they needed to talk to him again about your *kidnapping,* after they secured the scene and got what they could from the rest of the witnesses." He looked at her, regret in his cinnamon eyes. "By the time they came back to him, he'd disappeared. Hey." He took her hand, his fingers warm and strong around hers. "I'm sorry."

"You think those men took him?" She was beginning to feel light-headed. "They wouldn't hurt him, would they?"

He didn't say anything, just squeezed her hand, the car flying over the road. It was getting late, so that traffic was beginning to thin, not much standing in their way.

She pulled away to wrap her arms around herself. "He isn't my husband," she said at last, dazed.

"Boyfriend? I guess he's the father of your boys?"

She held Reid's somber gaze when he glanced over. Bit her lip. *Sooner or later...* It wasn't as if he wanted anything to do with them anyway. God, she'd been dreaming about this moment, wishing for this miracle for so long. And now that her most impossible dream had come true, nothing was as it should have been. It broke her heart.

She ignored the pain and filled her lungs. "No. You are," she told him.

Chapter Three

He almost drove into oncoming traffic. Reid eased off the gas and straightened the steering wheel, trying to get his racing mind under control. "This would not be the best time to mess with me."

She said nothing.

"How is that possible?" *Don't be an idiot,* he thought as soon as the words were out of his mouth, just as she said the exact same thing out loud.

He swallowed back a snappy response. Okay, so, yes, they'd done the necessary deed. But still, a pregnancy *wasn't* possible. But if he wasn't the father, then who was? Why wasn't he told that she was pregnant? He had asked for an update on her after he'd been evacuated from Hopeville. Someone had gone out, checked on her and reported back that she was fine.

Of course, her pregnancy might not have been showing at the time. The report had focused on the fact that her butcher shop had burned, too, but she'd received enough insurance money to rebuild. Not that he hadn't felt guilty anyway.

He stole a look at her from the corner of his eye and

decided to play along, figure out what her game was. "Which one?" She'd said Zak and Nate.

"Both. They're twins."

He gave a strangled cough as saliva went down the wrong way. He had to give it to her, when she did something, she really went to town with it. He loosened his hands on the steering wheel, which he'd been gripping so hard, his knuckles were beginning to ache.

"How did the fire start?" she asked.

And his muscles tightened again. "I can't talk about that."

Her voice deepened with anger. "I think you owe me an explanation."

Words she stole right out of his mouth. He waited a couple of seconds while he arranged his thoughts. He could give her the generalities. She did deserve something. "I was watching someone I suspected was a member of a group we had an interest in."

"We?"

He didn't respond.

"Law enforcement? Some government agency?"

"Something along those lines. Anyway, there was a leak somewhere. They figured out who I was. They came after me."

She was watching him, wide-eyed. "But then whose body was that in the ashes?"

Right. The body she had buried. An image rose in his mind—her standing by a headstone carved with his name. No reason he should feel bad about that—he'd just been doing his job—but he felt like a jerk anyway. "I took one of them out before they got to me."

That revelation silenced her for only a second. "How did you get out?"

"I wasn't as dead as they thought when they set the place on fire. I crawled off, called for help. The decision was made that it'd be best if I wasn't officially resurrected."

"You could have told me." Her voice was full of accusation.

"I was under orders not to. And the less you knew the safer you were." *The safer I was.*

If they'd spent any more time together, if he'd gone back… She would have become a complication. She would have made him vulnerable. He couldn't afford that. No weaknesses were allowed in his line of work. Soft spots had a way of turning deadly. He'd had to cut her off before she could come to mean too much to him.

She took a few seconds to digest his words. "Who were you watching?" she asked after a while.

He considered how much he could tell her. He was skating dangerously close to lines he should not cross. "Remember the gun shop across the strip mall?"

"Jimmy Sparks? Weird guy with the shaved head and the red goatee?"

He nodded.

"He closed shop and moved to Nevada right after the fire."

"Not exactly. He realized we were onto him and took

off. Location unknown." Along with his buddies. That whole operation had ended as a total bust, not one of his finest moments. It had taken two years of hard work to get this close again. And not a moment too soon. The cell was getting ready to pull off something major, after having practiced on single victims.

Reid hoped Jimmy would surface before it was all over. The two of them had a score to settle.

"Did he…kill anyone?" she asked, white-faced. "Why were you watching him?"

"He, um, made stuff." That was as much information as he was willing to divulge for now.

But she was quick on the uptake. "Oh. With his resources…" Her violet eyes went wide. She shook her head, muttering, "The butcher, the baker and the bomb maker," under her breath.

He couldn't help a pained grin. "A nursery rhyme for the twenty-first century, huh?"

She shook her head, looking dazed. "In Hopeville? It doesn't seem real."

Welcome to my world, he thought, but didn't say it. Truth was he didn't want her in his world. He wanted her as far from his world as could be arranged. The second she was bundled up with her kids in a safe house somewhere, he was putting as much distance between them as possible.

Now she knew he was alive. She could stop going to the damn cemetery. She had closure, or whatever she thought she needed. Best thing for her was to forget him.

THE REST OF THE TWO-HOUR drive from New York to Hopeville was spent mostly in silence, questions asked now and then and sparingly answered, both of them just trying to deal.

Reid called in once they were on her street. "I'm here. We're going in to get the kids. I want an invisible escort back to the highway, then I'm good. What did you find for me?" He memorized the address he was given. "Thanks."

He pulled into the driveway. "Stay." He got out, looked around, made two unmarked cop cars down the street. He nodded toward them and walked around to open the door for Lara. "Stick close to me. Everything looks quiet in there," he added, since she was almost vibrating with nervous energy.

She nodded and started forward, the first step a little shaky.

He cut in front of her, one hand on the gun in the back of his waistband. The door wasn't even locked. Small-town America. The kind of safe, idyllic life that was quickly disappearing, no matter how hard he and others like him fought to keep it going.

"I'm back," she called out from behind him, once he'd shoved the door open.

An elderly lady appeared from the kitchen, wearing pink sweatpants with a sweatshirt that had a kitten on the front, not someone he remembered from his brief stint in town. The woman didn't seem to recognize him either, which was all for the best. She gave him the once-over with a glint of disapproval in her squinty eyes. "I thought you were going with Allen?"

"Long story." Lara was hustling off toward the back of the house. She called over her shoulder, "Ran into an old friend."

"Hi," Reid said politely, cataloging as much of the house as he could see. While he'd known where Lara lived, he'd never been inside her home.

The place was small but tidy, toys neatly stacked in plastic bins. An old-fashioned model airplane hung from the ceiling. The sorriest-looking Christmas tree he'd ever seen stood in the corner, decorated with homemade ornaments, most of them color cutouts of a weird guy in a cape. The sign on his chest said Henry Hero. Probably the kids' favorite cartoon character.

He noted the furniture that was well worn, the carpet that had seen better days. When he'd heard that she'd gotten the insurance money, he'd figured she would be set. But now, knowing that she had to raise two small children alone, knowing that she'd paid for part of his funeral, he wondered, for the first time, whether things were tight for her. He didn't like the pang of guilt that came with that thought. In fact, he resented it.

She had come to him. But while that was true, there was also another truth in there somewhere. *He* could have, *should have,* sent her away. Strings of guilt twisted together with strings of lust, forming a rope that could bind him if he wasn't careful. He shook that rope off. He was not supposed to have any feelings, of any sort, where Lara Jordan was concerned.

"Well, I'll be going then." The babysitter nodded at him with a world of reservations, then called after Lara, "I'll take my payment in pork chops for Denis, as usual. I'll stop by the shop to see you. Allen likes chops, too. Did he tell you that? All alone in that big house of his. The man must be starved for a good, home-cooked meal."

"Okay," came from the back in a distracted tone. "Um, I might not be in the shop for a few days. I'm thinking about driving down to Florida to see my uncle."

"Bring back some sunshine if you go."

Reid stood by the window and looked after the old woman as she walked home down the street, her golden sneakers glittering. She glanced back from the corner to scowl at his SUV. Other than the waiting cops and the occasional passing car, nobody was out there.

Ten minutes didn't pass before Lara appeared, a car seat in each hand, two identical bundles inside. Between the blankets and the fuzzy hats, he didn't see much of the little sleeping faces. "Let me help."

She'd changed into jeans and a coat of her own, but had left on the Kevlar. She held out a car seat for him.

"I'll take the bag."

She set the baby on the couch so he could slide the enormous bag off her shoulder, and he noticed how tightly her full lips were pressed together, the worried shadows in her eyes.

"It's almost over. Stay behind me on the way out." He moved toward the door, looked out, stepped out, then signaled for her to follow.

He opened the back door of his car for her, let her secure the baby seats while he stashed her bag in the trunk. She was visibly shaken, but kept it together, efficient with the baby stuff. Then they were all in at last, and he got on the road, watching in the rearview mirror as the unmarked police cars followed them. In ten minutes, he was back on the highway and their escort fell back. In half an hour, he was crossing the state border to New York. The safe house, a small ranch home, wasn't far from there.

He found the key in the back, taped under the roof of the gazebo, as promised, and entered first, looked around and then motioned for her to follow. Two bedrooms, living room, kitchen, bathroom. Not much, but enough until he figured out what to do with her long term.

He had enough favors owed to him that he could put her into witness protection. *And never see her again.* A perfect solution for all involved. And yet, the thought didn't sit as well with him as it should have, especially considering that for some reason she was trying to con him. Because, despite her two little bundles of joy, which she was unwrapping in one of the bedrooms at the moment, the truth was, he couldn't have children. He'd known that for a fact since he'd been nineteen.

The question was, what did she have to gain by lying to him?

THE BOYS HAD WOKEN UP for a little while, but she'd been able to settle them back to sleep. They were good sleepers, the both of them, thank God. Otherwise, she didn't know how she could have managed as a single mother. She looked at their sweet baby faces. They were the most important things to her in the world. She would do anything to give them a happy, normal life, to keep them safe.

There was a time when she'd wanted to be wild and free. She'd been that, for a single night. Then the man she'd been infatuated with had died, her business had burned down and she'd become a single mother of twins, struggling to survive. She'd learned her lesson. She was done with adventure. All she wanted was an average, safe life. There was great comfort to be found in mediocrity.

She shored up the edge of the bed with pillows so the babies wouldn't roll off, then walked out, leaving the door slightly ajar.

Reid was sitting on the couch, legs apart, head back. Only one small light in the corner of the room was on, leaving his face shadowed and mysterious. He wore biker boots and faded jeans with an unbuttoned black shirt over his black T-shirt. She had a sudden flashback to the day she'd first seen him, appearing out of nowhere in the door of her shop, leaning against the frame and watching her, looking at her like no man ever had, before or since.

She'd been so stunned by the sight of him that she'd dropped ground pork into the ground beef bin. She should have turned tail right then and run for the hills.

Except, then she wouldn't have Zak and Nate, and she couldn't regret them, not ever, not for a second.

"Someone will bring us food." Reid stayed sprawled on the couch. "If you give me a list of what you need for your boys, I'll call it in."

"Our boys," she corrected.

He looked up at her with his cinnamon eyes narrowed, his thick lashes shading them. He had a chiseled face and lips that could... Lips that said he'd been born to be wild. "I don't think so."

Anger spread through her veins. "You think I'm lying about this?"

"I know you are. Look, I was going to give it some time and figure out why you're doing it, but I'm tired. There's a lot going on right now. I'll be leaving in a little while, handing you over to someone else. So let's cut through the games, and you tell me what you're up to."

"We slept together." She still thought about that night nearly every day. The possibility that he might have forgotten was humiliating.

But he said, "Believe me, I remember that part," his voice dropping a notch.

Heat crept into her face.

"But I'm telling you, honey, I can't have kids."

"Well, I'm telling you that you can, and you have," she snapped.

He watched her for a good long time, those piercing eyes doing their best to unnerve her. "I can't figure out the angle. Best I can come up with is that you had someone shortly after me, got pregnant, he took off and you told everyone the kids were mine since I was dead and I couldn't argue. Was he married?"

Anger progressed to cold fury. She strode into the kitchen for a glass of water. "Go to hell," she called back.

He came after her, turned her around by the shoulders, held her gaze and pulled up his T-shirt all the way to his neck.

Her throat went dry. She wanted to look away. She couldn't.

"Been there." His voice rasped. "And got the burn marks to prove it."

She swallowed a gasp at the sight of his mangled flesh. Blinked hard when she thought of the pure male perfection that he'd been the last time she'd seen his chest. All of that was gone now, angry, violent welts crisscrossing his skin.

For a moment, she forgot how mad she was at him for faking his death, for leaving her alone to deal with everything that came after, for denying their children. Her gaze slipped higher. "What's that on your shoulder?"

"This?" He flicked his thumb over the scar. "This is where my collarbone came through. The bastards broke a couple of bones before they set me on fire." He pulled his shirt down, covering it all.

And yes, he was still an unfair jerk for questioning her word about the twins, but the fight went out of her all of a sudden. This day and age, if he really wanted to know, paternity could be easily proven. But from what she'd seen of him so far, she didn't think she would want him in her life, in her babies' lives. She wanted safe and normal.

The good news was, he didn't look like he wanted to be part of her life either. He wouldn't even acknowledge their babies. One second she felt disappointment in that, the next she felt relief. She suspected she'd settle into relief once her mind calmed a little.

"The boys should be fine for a couple of days," she said. "I packed enough food and diapers for them. How long do you think we have to stay here? Tomorrow's Sunday so the shop isn't open, but if I can't come in Monday, I'll have to make arrangements." She had two part-time employees who could hold down the fort until her return.

"Make arrangements."

The unfairness of it all slammed into her. She'd done nothing wrong here. And yet, suddenly, her carefully built life was being ripped away. "So this is what you do?" she asked, full of resentment.

He nodded.

"Maybe you should have stuck with popovers and country bread. Couldn't you go back to something like that?"

"No."

Too bad. "You were better at that than this." She knew she sounded bitchy, and she didn't care.

He looked at her with interest. "How so?"

"Back in Hopeville, your cover got broken and you

were nearly killed. The same thing happened tonight." And both times, her life had changed as a result.

He gave a rueful smile. "Believe it or not, that's the only two times this ever happened to me. When you show up, everything falls apart. Maybe you're my personal bad luck charm." He gave a lopsided smile. "In fact, in the future, I'm planning on running in the opposite direction if you appear."

That stung. She stuck her chin out. "How about you start now?"

"Would be the smartest thing to do." He leaned closer, reached out and rubbed his thumb along the line of her jaw. "In fact, I'm planning on it as soon as backup gets here."

When he pulled away, she took a few nervous gulps of water. "Maybe you're *my* bad luck charm," she said as she set her glass down on the counter. "The first time you showed up in my life, my business burned down. Tonight I was shot at, and I had to go on the run with the boys because my home is no longer safe. *I* should run when I see *you* coming."

The way his gaze was focused on her lips made her warm all over. He moved back into her personal space again. "Run." His voice was a raspy whisper.

She couldn't have moved to save her life.

He grabbed her by the hips, lifted her onto the countertop effortlessly, settled his lean body between her legs. The sharp bolt of desire that shot through her took her breath away. What was it with them and food preparation surfaces?

"I'm not a sentimental person," he started, "but damn if memories aren't washing all over me. I can't say I like it."

"You could, uh, think about something else." She tried to get a grip on her hormones, which suddenly came awake after two long, exhausting, celibate years. "We were—that was so long ago, I already forgot all about it."

"I don't think so. I was your first," he whispered against her lips.

Awareness skittered across her skin.

"You must have had others since," he murmured, his lips a fraction of an inch from hers.

She turned her head, looked away.

He reached a finger under her chin and turned her back to him. "Allen?"

She shook her head. "Just you." How embarrassing. It wasn't as if she'd been pining for him all this time, but between the twins and the shop she'd had no time for torrid affairs.

"Liar," he said softly. His gaze darkened, something ferocious crossing his face, and then he claimed her lips with a passion that left her hanging on to his shoulders for dear life. Memories that had never fully faded came to life. But this wasn't like last time. This time, she didn't want this. She wasn't looking for any sort of adventure, especially with a man whose middle name was Bad News, a man who'd just called her a liar.

She put her hands between them, against his chest, and pushed weakly, her body warring with her mind.

She didn't think he would even feel her, but he stopped immediately and pulled back. Dark fires burned in his eyes.

His fingers loosened on her hips, then tightened again. He opened his mouth, but she didn't find out what he wanted to say. His ringing cell phone cut him off.

He answered it. "Hey." He listened, then closed it and slipped it back into his pocket. "Time for the changing of the guard."

She couldn't tell if the quick flash in his eyes was disappointment or relief.

REID WANTED TO USE the bathroom before he left, and on the way back out, he passed by the kids' room. A soft squeak came from inside. Sounded like they might be awake.

"Lara?" He could hear her talking with Ben, another guy from his unit who, like Reid, was on loan to the FBI, in the living room. Didn't respond. Probably didn't hear him.

He popped his head in the door with some reluctance. Maybe one of the kids just squeaked in his sleep, and wouldn't need her at all.

Only moonlight illuminated the room. He had to step closer to the bed to see. Two pairs of cinnamon eyes peered up at him.

"He, he," one of the boys said.

Strange kid. Without the hats and blankets, Reid could see them clearly now. And their faces were eerily familiar. Reid's mother had baby pictures of him that were nearly identical.

A bolt of lightning couldn't have hit him harder than his realization that Lara Jordan hadn't lied.

He didn't need a DNA test to know that Zak and Nate were really his.

He had kids. Kids he hadn't known about all this time. Two boys. And if she hadn't lied about that... Maybe he really was the only man she'd ever been with. The thought spread warmth through his chest in a way that was positively Neanderthal, but made him want to beat the stuffing out of Allen Birmingham a little less.

He should be angry. She'd just given him a weak spot a mile wide. He had a strategy that had worked for him so far. *Have nothing to lose.* It made him the meanest, baddest operative on the street. He never had to look back, never had to take his eyes off the prize. It was the only way to be the best in his field, and that was important to him. He was the job. The job was him.

Except that now Lara was back in his life. With twins.

He had to get out. He had to think.

He practically ran for the door.

But Lara spied him and ran after him. "Reid, wait."

He slowed with reluctance, turned back, his mind in turmoil. He couldn't deal with all this right now. He had to figure some things out for himself before he talked to her. And even before that, what he needed to do first was to find the damn CD Jen had talked about. Before the bad guys found it.

Lara looked a little lost as she wrapped her arms around herself, hesitant all of a sudden. "So, we— I suppose you won't be coming back." She glanced down at her feet.

Lara Jordan had his babies.

He moved back to her and touched her, against his better judgment, putting his crooked index finger under her chin and lifting her bottomless violet gaze to his. Against his better judgment, he allowed himself for the first time since he'd spotted her at the restaurant to notice how truly beautiful she looked. Against his better judgment, he allowed himself to admit how much he'd missed her.

He brushed his lips lightly across hers, smiling when her violet eyes opened wide with surprise. "I'll be back, honey. Count on it."

Chapter Four

Lara lay sleepless on the bed, listening to Zak's and Nate's soft breathing.

She'd already made all the necessary calls, letting everyone who needed to know that she would be away for a few days and had arranged coverage for the shop. She had nothing else to distract herself with.

Reid had resurrected.

They were all in danger.

A huge monkey wrench had just been thrown into her life. Again.

"We'll be fine as long as we have each other," she whispered to her little boys, trying to reassure both them and herself.

Zak opened his eyes. "He, he," he said sleepily.

"There's no Henry Hero here," she soothed him. That was the boy's favorite cartoon. She didn't let them watch much TV, but they usually begged her for Henry Hero.

If Reid didn't want anything to do with them, it was his loss. He'd lit out of the house like a bat out of hell.

But he was coming back. She wasn't sure if she should look forward to that or be scared.

Tears burned her eyes. He was Reid Graham, but not *her* Reid Graham.

Two years ago, she'd only known him for a short while. Enough to develop a thorough infatuation, but not nearly enough to truly get to know him. And, in the aftermath of his death, she had filled in the blanks.

She'd fancied that although he was rough around the edges, he had a golden heart. He'd become her imaginary gentle giant. A biker baker who was just waiting for the chance to become a family man.

Right.

The reality was that he was some sort of ruthless undercover operative, the kind of man who got involved in shoot-outs, someone who probably lived for danger, someone who had been able to walk away from her without a backward glance. Someone who couldn't care less that they had two beautiful baby boys together.

It was this last thought that just about broke her heart. Because her babies deserved better.

She had no idea where he had gone, and she had no idea when he would be back. *If* he came back. In his line of work, she didn't think she could take his return for granted, no matter what he'd promised. If they had a life together, this was what it would be like, not an epic love affair and running their businesses together and raising their family, as it had been in her dreams.

God, she couldn't believe she'd been so stupid.

She squeezed her eyes shut, but sleep wouldn't come.

And if she kept tossing and turning, she would eventually wake the twins. She could hear Ben moving around in the living room. She got up and went out to see what he was doing.

The man's head came up. "Everything okay in there?"

She nodded.

He was a little shorter than Reid, more gangly. And beyond handsome in his own right, with lively blue eyes that didn't miss anything. No tattoos that she could see. He was a more clean-cut type of guy. Could pass for a stockbroker on Wall Street if he put on a three-piece suit. He was pretty close to her age, she guessed. Probably a half dozen years younger than Reid.

He was studying a detailed map of the neighborhood on his laptop. Probably planning escape routes, or whatever it was that people like him did in situations like this.

She sank onto the couch. "Are you married?" She winced, embarrassed, as soon as the words were out. She really needed to start thinking before she spoke. "I mean, I was wondering what your wife thinks when you take off for parts unknown in the middle of the night."

"Single." He focused his gaze on her. "Interested?"

She had to laugh at the immediate, flattering response. "I have my hands full at the moment, but thanks for offering."

He shrugged, and said in a voice underscored with

regret, "Just as well. You're a pretty hot babe, but going up against Reid would be dicey."

"Reid and I are not like that." For the moment, she was ignoring the kisses they'd shared. They couldn't have meant anything to him. He was the kiss-and-leave type. Definitely. That she was still attracted to him, even knowing who and what he really was, was beyond her understanding, so she opted for denial—as far as that went.

A dark blond eyebrow slid up Ben's forehead. "From the way he was looking at you… Could have fooled me." He gave a quick grin. "There's more tension between you two than at a hostage exchange."

"That's, um… We have a kind of history."

Ben kept grinning.

"Which is over," she said with all the self-confidence she could muster.

"Whatever you say, babe."

And that made her laugh. She was almost six feet tall, and built like a butcher, for sure. Nobody had ever called her babe.

Reid called her honey. She was so not going to think about that. "So you work with Reid a lot?"

Ben went back to the map, as if he hadn't even heard her.

"Let me guess, if you told me anything about your job, you'd have to kill me."

He looked up, amusement dancing in his blue eyes. "Or make you my sex slave and ravish you until you could think of nothing but my body, forgetting everything else. It's the kind of mind control we practice."

And she knew she was in trouble. Because here was a really hot guy, talking dirty to her. At the very least, she should have felt a *zing*. But she felt nothing. She wished Reid had come back already. "On second thought, maybe you should keep your secrets."

Again, Ben returned to the map, muttering something under his breath that sounded like, "Damn Reid."

Not a second passed before he raised his head and became deathly still, the smile sliding off his face.

Her heart rate picked up in response to the sudden tension in the air. "What is it?"

Gun in hand, he was moving toward the window. "Turn off the light. Go back to the kids. Lock the door."

She didn't ask questions, but did as she was told. She even wedged a chair under the doorknob for good measure. Then she lay down next to Zak and Nate, shielding them with her body.

For several minutes, she could hear nothing but the babies breathing and the blood rushing loudly in her ears. Then a small pop sounded at the back door. A gunshot? Silencer? Her breath about stopped. Then she shook herself. What did she know about silencers? Only what she'd seen in movies. No need to get fanciful. *Stay calm. No reason to panic.* Then another pop came, and another. The floor creaked. A door was slammed open. There were people in the house.

Definitely reason to panic. She slid off the bed.

Scanned the room for a weapon. Nothing in here but the bed and the dresser. The worst she could do to anyone who entered was to engage him in a pillow fight, for heaven's sake. But she wasn't giving up without trying. She couldn't let her babies down.

One thing she knew for sure was that if the attackers came in, she was toast. She and the boys had to get out of here. She moved to the window, took care to slide it open as quietly as possible. Cold air blew in immediately. She was on her way to wrap Zak and Nate up in the blanket and get out when the door was kicked open, the chair bouncing off the opposite wall, breaking into splinters.

Zak and Nate woke up at the same time and started crying.

"Shut the hell up," the man who filled the doorway barked, his face covered by a black ski mask.

Another masked guy was right behind him.

REID STOOD IN THE MIDDLE of Jen's apartment, the guilt he felt over her death intensifying. She'd been his asset. He should have protected her. He tried to dig down to his customary cold logic, the one that would tell him that she'd been a member of a terrorist cell. She'd tortured and killed people alongside her boyfriend. She had put herself in the path of danger when she'd hooked up with the likes of Kenny Briggs.

Except that when she found out she was pregnant, she'd decided to get the hell out of Dodge, putting out feelers for turning evidence in exchange for money and protection.

She would have gotten both. She and her kid could have lived happily ever after. If Reid's personal life hadn't intersected with his job at that precise moment, for the first time in many, many years. And like the last time, the result was a disaster.

This was exactly why the job always had to come first, personal life second. Or rather, with him, the job came first, second and third, and he hadn't allowed a personal life at all. Except that now, personal matters were forcing their way into his life. He had to figure out what to do about that before anyone else died. He had to contain a looming disaster.

And the first step toward that goal was to completely shut Lara and the babies out of his mind and focus one hundred percent on finding Jen's CD.

Jen's place had been tossed before he'd gotten there. He didn't think whoever had done this had found what they were looking for. The mess was apocalyptic, as if they'd ripped the place apart searching, then trashed it in frustration at the end.

So where had Jen hidden the damned thing?

He stood still, closed his eyes and in his mind ran through his whole conversation with Jen at the restaurant. Couldn't pick out a single clue. So he ran the conversation again. This time, his subconscious got snagged on a sentence.

"My sister knows," Jen had said, referring to her pregnancy.

According to her file, Jen was estranged from her family. They didn't see eye to eye with Kenny and the values he represented. Jen had cut her family off three years ago to devote all her time and energy to Kenny and his buddies, to the *cause*.

So when had she made up with her sister? Eileen was the name, he thought. He was dialing his FBI handler as he headed back to his car.

"Hey. The asset we lost tonight… Her apartment was trashed. Send someone out here for fingerprints. See if the neighbors noticed anyone coming and going and maybe have a description. Can you get into her police file right now? Okay. I need her sister's address." He memorized the information. "I'll call if I have anything."

He was in a cutesy cul-de-sac near Philly less than two hours later, bungalow houses that were probably thirty, forty years old lined the street, each sitting on about a fifth of an acre. He pulled into the driveway of a house with the number he'd been looking for. The lights were on.

Which meant he couldn't push in a back window and investigate on his own. He would have to ask permission. Because he sure as hell didn't have time to wait for a warrant.

He got out of the car, walked up to the door and knocked. It was seven in the morning.

A red-eyed woman opened the door. She was a few years older than Jen had been, same color irises, different color hair. She was clutching a wad of tissues in her hand.

"Good morning, ma'am. I'm Reid Graham. I know I'm coming at a bad time, but I need to ask some questions about your sister."

Tears welled. "I already told everything to the detective." She swallowed a sob, pressing the wad of tissues to her nose.

She assumed that he was another cop, like the one who'd come to inform her of her sister's death, and he didn't correct her. The assumption worked fine for him.

"We've had some developments since," he said simply.

That did the trick. She motioned him in.

The house was as modest inside as it was outside, clean and well-kept, like Lara's place. Except this home was decorated within an inch of its life with ribbons and ruffles, a Victorian medley of roses and lace that made him dizzy. The Christmas decorations were equally overwhelming and exuberant. He sat in a pink flowery armchair—accented with a red-and-white candy-cane patterned throw and matching decorative pillow—refusing to let it intimidate him.

She sagged onto the couch, which was smothered in Christmas pillows. "Do you know who killed her?"

"Not yet."

"I told the other detective that she was running with bad people. Kenny, her boyfriend… Creepy guy. Even violent." She sniffed.

"We're certainly investigating that angle. Could you tell me when you last saw your sister?"

"Yesterday." The word brought a new batch of tears. "We haven't really talked in years. She showed up out of the blue. She said she regretted running off with Kenny. I called Mom right after she left. We were so happy that she came to her senses. She was going to have a baby." Eileen gave a loud sob.

"How long was she here?"

"She was in a hurry. I shouldn't have let her go. Oh, God, if I only knew…"

"Can you tell me exactly what she did while she was here, what rooms she went into, everything she touched?"

A few rapid blinks came. "Why?"

"I have reason to believe that she left something here."

"She didn't."

"She wouldn't have told you."

Eileen's back stiffened. "But I would have seen her."

"Mind if I look anyway? If I'm right, the evidence can put her killer away for a long time. And it can save the lives of many others."

Eileen hesitated for only a second before she nodded. Then she stood and walked toward a hall closet. "Jen came in. She took her coat off. I put it in the closet for her."

"Mind if I check?"

"Go ahead."

He rifled through coat pockets, even checked inside boots. Then he pulled out a large, brown purse and handed it to Eileen. "Would you look through it to make sure there's nothing in there that shouldn't be?"

She did as he asked, shook her head when she was done. "Just the things I always carry."

"Thank you. What did she do after she came in?"

"We had coffee." She led the way to the kitchen. "She sat here."

He checked all the drawers within arm's length. Nothing. "And then?"

"We talked a little. She was nervous. And then she left."

"Are you sure?"

Eileen nodded. But then she said, "She used the bathroom first." She pointed down the hallway.

He strode into the small space, looked around. A pine-scented candle burned in the window. Nothing seemed out of place. He looked in the medicine cabinet. It held the usual: makeup and pills, toothbrushes. Nothing but cleaning supplies under the sink. He picked through the garbage, even looked under the trash-can liner. Nothing. He looked under a snowman-patterned floor mat. Nothing. He opened the tank. Empty, save for water.

Dammit.

He needed the information on that CD. He glanced at his watch. It was close to 8:00 a.m., Sunday. He had six days until Christmas. Every instinct he had said that whatever attack Kenny's group was planning was going to come on Christmas Day. Their communications had become more and more frequent as the holidays approached. There was a marked increase in their phone and Internet activity. The cell leader's identity was unknown. The FBI had a list of foot soldiers, but had determined that picking any of them up would gain little information while resulting in increased security within the cell, putting them on guard. Only the men at the very top would know the exact details of the attack. They'd keep everyone else in the dark until the very last moment to prevent a leak.

Kenny Briggs, however, had earned a promotion not that long ago, according to an informant who'd dropped off the face of the earth since his last report. Unfortunately, the FBI hadn't been able to find him for further questioning. Neither could they find Kenny. He kept slipping through their fingers.

Reid had been counting on Jen's CD.

They'd been this close before. In Hopeville they'd almost had Jimmy Sparks, another thug who'd worked his way up in the cell. But then Reid's cover had been blown and Jimmy had disappeared. He couldn't let that happen again.

He was ready to turn when his eyes caught on the open toilet lid. It was decorated with a fuzzy toilet cover, held in place by a circle of elastic. He closed the lid, pulled the cover off—same snowman pattern as the bathmat.

"Hot damn," he whispered under his breath.

"You found it?" Eileen's eyes were round with surprise when he came back to her.

"Lucky for everyone involved. I need your permission to take it, or I'll have to call in for a warrant."

"You can take it."

Of course, he still had to have her sign a form giving him permission to take custody of the evidence. Luckily, he had just such a form in his pocket. He'd taken one to the meeting with Jen, in case she had something for him. Never got around to having her sign it for that cell phone. Which was now with Ben. Ben was a whiz with everything electronic. He could break the code and download the call history from the cell, even if it had been deleted.

He whipped out the sheet and slid it on the counter. "Would you sign here?"

Five minutes later, he was in his car, heading away from Philly, talking on his phone to Mark Adams, his FBI handler. "I have the CD. I need someone to meet me and pick it up. Then I'm heading back to the safe house. As soon as you have the info from the CD, you can send it over there for me. I'll ask Ben to leave his laptop."

"Good work, Graham. Where are you?"

He gave his location.

"Okay. Take the next exit. Pull over at the back of the truck stop. What car do you have?"

He gave make, model and license plate.

"I'll have someone there to pick up the evidence in an hour. And, hey, the Allen guy you were asking about was found. Apparently, he was shaken up and went out back for a smoke. Then he had a panic attack or something and passed out. He's fine now. They let him go home."

He called Ben's cell phone next to check up on them. The line was busy. He had call waiting, so he'd know Reid was trying to check in. If he couldn't talk now, he'd call back later. And he remembered that he hadn't called out for food before he'd left. They'd probably gotten hungry. Ben was probably ordering.

He tossed the phone on the passenger seat and took the next exit. Once he'd pulled behind the truck stop, there was nothing to do but wait, which did little for his resolution to not think about Lara and the babies.

Over the years, he'd talked himself into believing that she hadn't meant any more to him than the others, that there hadn't been anything special between them. The last couple of hours had blasted that nice, comfortable facade to hell.

Dammit.

He should have known all along. If she hadn't been anyone special, he wouldn't have broken all the rules and slept with her in the first place. If she didn't mean more than the others, he could have forgotten her over the past two years. The truth was, he had little power to resist, and even less good judgment when it came to Lara Jordan.

Otherwise, he wouldn't have kissed her tonight in the safe house's kitchen.

Otherwise, he would now be thinking of nothing but the job, instead of wishing for impossible things.

Getting distracted was the very best way to get both of them killed. He wouldn't have it. They had a past. A past that had more to it than he'd thought. *Zak and Nate.*

That had been a shock. He could have kids. At some point, he needed to sit down and think about the implications of that. His life was partially based on the assumption that he would never be a family man, never be a father. He was now. A father. To twins.

Well, he was the worst person ever to attempt to raise kids. He'd never be around, for one. Two, his job was dangerous. What if someone figured out that he had a family? What if they decided to use his family to get to him?

Having any kind of relationship in the future with Lara and the boys was out of the question. For their sake.

He would help financially. Through a third party. Make sure the money couldn't be traced. That was the best thing he could do. That was the safest thing he could do.

Logic said he needed distance.

A dull ache deep inside his chest said something else. He decided to ignore that ache.

It wasn't like he would miss them. The very thought was completely illogical. He barely knew Lara and he didn't know the boys at all. You couldn't miss people you didn't know.

The pickup car's arrival interrupted his musings. The agent showed ID. Signed for the evidence. Bagged it properly.

Then Reid was on his way back to the safe house. His mind swam with all the thoughts and questions he had regarding those kids. Lara and he needed to have a good, long talk about this.

He picked up his phone to call Ben again to make sure that everything was okay, but it rang before he could dial.

"Have you heard from Ben?" Adams asked.

"I was just about to call him."

"He's not answering his phone. Gunshots were reported in the neighborhood. Local law enforcement is on the way."

He closed the phone and tossed it on the passenger seat, stepped on the gas and shot down the highway, ignoring when horns blared all around him. The very thing he wanted to avoid the most—Lara and the boys in danger because of him—had already become reality. *Dammit.*

He was at least thirty minutes away. Even as the needle on the speedometer climbed up, he knew he'd be too late.

Chapter Five

The drive to the safe house was the longest of his life. He'd been tortured before, brutally, when the pain that seemed to have no beginning and no end had the power to bring time to a standstill. Now, as then, the seconds ticked away with a desperate, agonizing slowness that drove him crazy.

It was nearly noon by the time he was finally flying down the right street. The sight of cop cars and two ambulances by the curb was enough to make him go gray. He pulled over and jumped from his car, burst into the house—and nearly got shot.

"Reid Graham, I'm with the FBI." He flashed his temporary badge as guns pointed at him. "Where are they?"

The two officers inside the living room lowered their weapons, scowling at him for causing unnecessary excitement.

"Your man?" one of them asked, gesturing to the corner.

Ben, unconscious, lay on the floor, a pool of blood

under his head. Half of one ear was missing. Looked like he was shot from behind.

Anger twisted through Reid. "How is he?"

"Massive head trauma," an EMT said without looking up as they transferred Ben onto a waiting stretcher. "But if he makes it to the hospital he has a chance."

"The woman and the babies?" Reid demanded.

Then Lara's broken voice came from somewhere in the rear of the house, and his heart gave a hard thud. He pushed his way past the men as they rolled the stretcher out. In the hall, another officer was coming from the babies' room. Reid identified himself again. The man nodded and kept going, letting him pass.

The first thing he saw in the small bedroom was another EMT. Then the man shifted, and Reid spotted Lara sitting on the bed, a large bruise on her cheek. She looked catatonic, her eyes staring but not seeing, tears shining on her checks, trying to get away from the man who was treating her.

No babies.

Some people reacted to strong emotions like fear and anger by blowing up like a volcano. Reid had a stone-cold rage that others sometimes mistook for calmness, missing the killer instinct behind the controlled facade. He held strong and still, when what he wanted to do was tear the whole damn house apart. But he would wait and focus his powers of destruction until he found the men who were responsible. Then God help the bastards.

"Lara?" He stepped closer.

The EMT was treating lacerations on her knuckles

and wrists with one hand, holding her on the bed with the other. "Take it easy. I wish you'd lie down, ma'am."

She didn't say a word, just tried to get past him. If she weren't so drugged, she would have evaded him, but as it was, her movements were too slow and uncoordinated.

"How is she?" Reid's control kept his voice even.

The EMT glanced at him for a split second before focusing back on his work, wrapping gauze around Lara's wrist. "They tied her up. Wounds are mostly superficial, but she'll have to keep them clean to prevent infection."

Reid pushed back the rage a sliver, surprised when an overwhelming tenderness immediately filled the void. He moved forward to kneel next to her, put a hand on her arm to hold her in place. "Lara, honey?"

She stilled and slowly lifted her gaze to him, her expression tortured. "They took Zak and Nate."

"I know, honey." He squeezed her hand.

"It's your fault! You brought us here." She shook him off. "Don't you *honey* me." Her words held a tigress's growl.

The EMT started tending to the rope burns on her ankles.

Reid sat next to her on the bed and pulled her to his chest, rested his chin on the top of her head. "Hey, nobody messes with my boys. I'll find them. You better believe it."

But she didn't seem to hear him. She tugged free. "I

begged them to take me, too. Why wouldn't they take me? I want to be with my babies."

He put a hand on her arm to hold her on the bed. "Did they tell you anything? A message to give me?"

"The taller one said you had to hang on to some CD." She tried to yank her arm out of his grip. "If anything happens to the twins because of your stupid job, I swear to God, Reid—"

"You need help over there?" The cop was coming back to check on them.

"I got her." He held her firmly, but at the same time made sure she wouldn't hurt herself with her incessant tugging. "Any clues as to who the attackers were and where they went?"

"Nothing. The ambulance is leaving with your buddy," the officer told Reid. "You want to go with him?"

"I'm staying. But I want to be notified when he regains consciousness."

The cop gave a brief nod before disappearing from the doorway.

The EMT patted his handiwork and stood. "That should do it. She needs to rest as much as possible." He flashed Reid a pointed look.

Of course, even now, she was swatting his hands away, trying to get away from him. "Bad news," she mumbled.

And while the EMT probably didn't know what she was talking about, Reid did. She was talking about him. He was the bad news in her life, bringing nothing but pain, over and over again. He didn't protest her words. He agreed wholeheartedly. And the fact that he had brought trouble to her door once again was killing him.

He stepped in front of the door to block her from leaving the room on the EMT's heels, then pulled his cell phone out.

"Who are you calling?" Even the question was spoken in a tone of accusation.

"Backup. I need you to be taken someplace else while I look for Zak and Nate." *And skin anyone alive who laid a finger on them.* The veneer that held him in check was wearing awfully thin.

"Like hell." She stepped up to him. "Do you hear me? I'm going after the twins. I'm going with you. If you dare leave me, I'll just get away. I'll follow you." She stabbed him in the chest with her index finger. "I can do it."

The desperation underlying her anger came through in her voice and twisted his guts.

He closed the phone and pulled her hard against his chest. His arms tightened around her on their own. Truth was, he didn't want to leave her. He didn't want to let her out of his sight. He didn't want to let her out of his arms. *Ever.* And because that thought unsettled him, he dropped his arms away from her.

"Sit on the bed. Let me think," he ordered.

She did, probably knowing he was about to give in.

A cell phone rang in the living room. When nobody picked it up after several rings, he strode out to get it.

Through the window, he could see the cops combing the front lawn, casting tire molds. He grabbed the cell phone from the coffee table—Kenny's backup phone that Jen had passed on to Reid, then Reid had passed on to Ben.

"Hey," he answered, hoping someone was calling Kenny, hoping he could fake his way through the conversation and come away with something usable.

But the call was for him.

"We got the kids. You got the CD. Let's trade."

Everything inside him went cold. "Say when and where." He wasn't about to let on that he had nothing to negotiate with.

"I'll be calling you," the voice said, and then the line went dead.

He swore a blue streak.

"What is it?" Lara was coming from the bedroom because, of course, she wouldn't stay put. Her gaze went to the pool of blood on the dingy carpet. She blinked hard. "How is Ben?"

"He's a tough bastard. You're not to worry about him." She had plenty on her mind without starting to feel guilty now that someone had gotten hurt protecting her and her babies. Ben had known the risks when he'd signed on. This was the kind of job they both did. When you were on protection detail, you were paid to step in front of bullets, not hide from them.

"Who called?" Lara was asking.

He flexed his jaw to keep it from clenching. "The woman who was killed at the restaurant was supposed to give me something. They want it in exchange for Zak and Nate."

"You have to give it to them." She charged at him on unsteady legs. "Whatever it is..."

"I already passed it off." *How much sedative had that idiot EMT given her?*

"Tell whoever you're working for to give it back," she demanded, then wrapped her arms around herself and swore like a commando soldier. Which was a first. He'd never heard her say words like that before. A whole new Lara, definitely.

"They won't. The people I work for don't negotiate with terrorists."

She swayed, all the blood running out of her face. He caught her, hating to see her all drugged up like this. He picked her up and carried her to the couch, ignoring her uncoordinated attempts to get away from him. He practically had to sit on her to keep her from running while he dialed his phone and spoke.

"They just took Ben to the hospital. Doesn't look good. I have Miss Jordan. Both babies are missing." Saying the words out loud seemed to amplify the emptiness in his chest. He rubbed a fist against his breastbone.

"Got anything?" Adams asked on the other end.

"Ben was in no condition for a debriefing. The EMT had to sedate Miss Jordan. I'll talk to her as soon as the drugs wear off. I got a call on Kenny's cell. I'll call you from that in a minute so you have the number. See if you can trace all incomings and outgoings for the last couple of days. The bastards think Jen gave me that CD. They want a trade."

"They can want it all day long. We don't do exchanges with terrorists. Any negotiations will be conducted by our special hostage negotiators. That CD is staying exactly where it is."

Reid let the CD thing slide for the moment, with every intention of getting his hands on it one way or the other.

"Any idea how they found the safe house in the first place?" Adams was asking.

He'd thought about that on the way here in the car. He picked up Kenny's cell now from the coffee table, and turned it over in his hand. "I'm guessing the phone Jen gave me has some kind of a locator. Could be Kenny didn't trust her. Or Kenny's boss, whoever that is, didn't trust Kenny. Someone was trying to keep tabs on someone and, by accident, ended up having our location."

A moment of silence. "Maybe the cell leader has locators in the cell phones of the others. Somehow they figured out that Jen was defecting. Went to the restaurant to see who she was meeting with. Tried to take both of you out. You escaped, and they realized that you had the phone."

"Which led them straight here." Pretty much the theory he had come up with. His muscles tightened as he thought of the danger he'd put Lara and the babies in. He was too dangerous for them to be around. Once he found the boys, he would make sure that he set them up as far away from him as possible.

Here came that chest pain again. Once more, he rubbed it away.

"Lara Jordan's name is in your file," his handler said, his voice carefully neutral.

Which set off all kinds of warning bells. Reid stiffened. He was SDDU, Special Designation Defense Unit, a covert commando group that worked mostly abroad. He'd been investigating a terrorist training camp in the mountains of Afghanistan when he'd discovered a U.S. link that had led him back stateside to a domestic cell here. Since the FBI was already investigating them, contact was made with the Bureau. And somehow they'd talked Colonel Wilson, the man who ran the SDDU, into loaning Reid out to them.

He wasn't used to anyone being able to see his file. Then he realized Adams couldn't possibly be referring to his SDDU file. The FBI had to have their own file on him. And since he'd worked on the Hopeville case with them—although with another handler—of course, they would have that information.

"I know her from the Hopeville operation," he said, information they obviously already had.

"Are you the father of those children?" came the next question.

Okay, so they'd done the math. Maybe it would have been smarter to say no, but he found that he couldn't deny his boys again. "Yes." And he needed to get them back ASAP. "I want that CD."

"No can do. This is too important."

"So are my boys, dammit!"

Adams wasn't giving him anything. He'd always been a cold bastard, the type to never bend. Reid had always hated that, but never more than now, when something personal was at stake.

"You know the drill. It's two lives against the lives of hundreds or possibly thousands. I'm not going to make any rash decisions here. *If* there's an exchange, we'll be handling it. As I said, we have professional negotiators for times like this. People who aren't personally involved in the case."

The only reason Reid didn't tell Adams where he could shove his professional negotiators was because he'd expected exactly that answer. *Keep cool, come up with another plan.*

"I want those bastards," he said, because it was the truth, and because Adams would get suspicious if he gave up without protest.

"And you can't have them. You're too emotionally involved in this. You're off the case."

Which wasn't completely unexpected either. Not that the lack of surprise made accepting the words any easier. But Reid knew the system well enough to know that arguing would be futile. He also knew the system well enough to know how to play it.

"I want to keep guarding Miss Jordan. She already knows me. She's comfortable with me. It'll keep me out of the way." Remaining civil practically killed him, but he got the words out somehow.

Adams hesitated. "In light of all that you've done for us, okay. Yes."

"I appreciate it. I have a place nobody knows about. I'll take her there once she's had a chance to settle down a little." He rolled his shoulders to relax them. "So what's on the CD?"

"Being worked on as we speak."

"Bob?" He knew the resident code cracker, Bob Barnaby. They'd worked together on the Hopeville case. "Let me know as soon as you have anything."

"If you promise to stay put and stay out of trouble." Silence again. "Look, I know this is hard for you. I have a daughter. I didn't even know you..."

"Yeah. Me, neither."

"That's tough. Must have been a hell of a surprise."

He wasn't about to discuss that with Adams. "You just do whatever it takes to get them back."

"You bet."

He ended that call then rang Adams from Kenny's phone so the FBI would have that number and could start investigating. Ben must have gotten started on it, but he had no idea what the man had learned so far.

"Okay, this is it. Whatever you find, let me know," he told Adams. Then he hung up and took Kenny's phone apart, found the transmitter, removed it and put it in the ashtray in the middle of the table. He switched to his own phone when he was done with that, and made another call.

"Hey, Carly. I have a favor to ask." He didn't have to identify himself—his SDDU code on Carly's display would do that. She was also a member of the unit.

"Shoot."

"The FBI is working on a CD. I need a copy. The guy whose account you're looking for once you hack into Quantico's mainframe is Bob Barnaby."

"Piece of cake." Carly chuckled into the phone. "Want me to get the cure for cancer while I'm at it? Have I ever mentioned that I'm kind of attached to the idea of seeing my kids graduate from kindergarten? I mean in person, not from pictures while I sit in federal prison."

"I wouldn't ask if there were another way. My boys were kidnapped."

A moment of silence on the other end. "Are you playing with me? Are you dangling an irresistible challenge in front of my nose as a joke? Because if you are, Reid Graham, I'm coming to get you. And you're not going to like it when I get there."

She was a pro at sounding like the queen of mean, one woman he would have hated to count among his enemies.

"You don't have kids. So what is this about?" she drilled him.

"Fourteen-month-old twins, Zak and Nate. Long story."

"I bet." The voice had a smile in it now. "All right, you sly dog. But when this is over, I want to hear all about it. And I do mean details."

He could hear clicking on the other end. She was on her laptop already.

"I'll call you when I have anything," she promised.

He set his phone down, his guts twisting. "I'll bring them back," he told Lara, who'd just about gotten free.

He pulled her back, onto his lap, against his better judgment, and put his arms around her.

Normally, he wasn't the snuggling kind. He couldn't say he'd ever wanted to just hold a woman. And if emotional upheaval was at hand, he usually ran for the nearest exit. But he needed to be holding her now. Ironic because she didn't seem to be able to get away from him fast enough.

He let her go with a sigh after a few unsatisfactory moments.

"Why did you tell those people that you're the boys' father?" she demanded. "I thought you didn't believe me."

"I was an idiot before. I'm sorry." He hesitated. He wasn't the type of guy who discussed his past, as a rule, ever. Partially that came from his job, partially from his personality. But as he looked into her eyes, he felt he owed her an explanation.

"Look, about a million years ago when I was a young pup, I had this older girlfriend. She had a kid already. She wanted another. We gave it a good try. Nothing happened. I figured since she already had a kid—" He shrugged.

"You thought something was wrong with you."

"Then a couple of years back, I had a wife." He pushed away those dark memories. He didn't want to think of Leila's broken body, the grave on the side of that damned mountain in Afghanistan where he'd buried her. "Anyway, nothing happened there either. So I was pretty sure.

"Plus there was this other thing. I caught some shrapnel to a sensitive area at one point."

"Ouch."

"You're telling me. So the doctor said I might have, you know, trouble from that later."

Her red-rimmed eyes blinked. "You had a wife?" She stared at him, storm clouds gathering on her face.

"Long story." He definitely wasn't going to talk about that. To anyone. Ever.

She took a wobbly step back. "While you were in Hopeville?" Another layer of hurt was added to her voice, her violet eyes widening with the pain.

Okay, so he hadn't always been truthful with her. Still, it stung that she was so ready to assume the worst about him. "I'm a conscienceless bastard for the most, but not that much of a bastard. A vote of confidence would be nice here."

Her eyes narrowed. "You've been lying to me from the get-go. I'm not going to apologize. What happened to her?"

"She was killed." Along with two hundred forty-two innocent men, women and children—most of a small Afghan village. Because of him.

REID WAS HER ONLY HOPE, and he was the most terrible last resort a desperate woman could have, Lara thought as the drugs wore off. Hours had passed while the two of them waited for a call, some clue they could follow. He wasn't just bad luck for her, he was bad luck for all women, it seemed. He'd had a wife. And she'd been killed. He hadn't said that it'd been his fault, but the look on his face told a grim story. His face had been so hard she thought his cheekbones would crack.

She wondered whether his tragic marriage happened before or after he'd come to Hopeville to mess up her life forever. It didn't matter. She had little claim on him. And still, when she thought of him walking away from Hopeville, leaving her behind, heartbroken and pregnant, to marry another woman, her heart twisted with pain.

"Will you tell me about her?" She bit her lip. It wasn't like her to be a masochist. Maybe he wouldn't answer. God, she needed to get out of here. She moved away from him, walking to the hall closet for her coat.

"No."

And she nodded, equally disappointed and relieved.

He came around her to block the front door. "And you're not going anywhere. How are you feeling?" He searched her face.

"Better. My heart is still ripped out, but the drugs are wearing off, so at least I can think. You can't expect me to sit still here." It was midafternoon. She couldn't stand the thought of all those hours her babies had already spent without her.

"So what, you're planning a statewide house-to-house search? They can be anywhere. Before we act, we need information to act on. I know waiting is pain—"

His cell phone rang.

"Thanks. I owe you one," he said to whoever was

calling. Then he walked over to Ben's laptop on the coffee table.

She followed, needing to know what information was coming in.

He opened his e-mail. He had a single message in his otherwise empty inbox. She must have had ten thousand in her own. Maybe he never saved anything, as a security measure.

The sender field was blank. The message said, *Here is the first file. Still working on the rest.*

She watched over his shoulder as he opened the attachment and scrolled through information that meant little to her. "What is it?"

"The ingredient list for some kind of chemical compound." He scrolled some more. "No, never mind. That's just the carrying agent." His finger stopped on the keyboard. "Oh, hell."

"What?"

"PX12. A virus originally engineered as a bioweapon by our own fine government. Then abandoned when it proved to be too difficult to control."

"How deadly is it?" she barely dared to ask.

"Enough to take out a couple of thousand people by New Year's if it's released at Christmas. And as it's passed on… By Easter, we're talking about a hundred thousand deaths."

She sat suddenly, the strength going out of her knees. She'd suspected that he was involved in something pretty bad, something she didn't even want to know about. But this was worse than she'd thought. And now her babies were in the middle of it. She couldn't breathe all of a sudden. "When?" she asked, stunned. "Where?"

"That's the million-dollar question. Let's hope there's information about that in one of the other files. In the meantime, I know someone who might know more about this stuff." He pulled out his cell phone and dialed.

"Hey. I'm going to read you a list of nasties. Can you tell me who handles this stuff in the New York–Philly area?" He read the list of ingredients for the carrying agent then waited for the answer. "That's fine. Call me back when you have it."

He stood to stretch his legs, his expression thoughtful, as if he were searching through a catalog of information in his head, trying to look for something, anything, that would give them a clue, a connection. He was calm, but not relaxed. More like the complete silence of the land before a major earthquake or other natural disaster. There was something foreboding in the way he measured his steps.

She walked out to the kitchen for a glass of water, her mouth dry as baby powder. Side effect of the drugs she'd been given, no doubt. Now that they'd worn off, panic was gripping her muscles again, nothing dulling the pain that seared through her chest. She felt hollow without her babies, empty. She took a long drink. It didn't help. Her hands began to shake. She was losing it.

"I can't stand the waiting." She slammed the plastic cup on the counter. She couldn't stand thinking how scared Zak and Nate must be without her.

"We won't be sitting around much longer. The second

we have something to go on, we're out of here." He looked at the e-mail on his laptop again, then back at her. "So here are the ground rules. When I say duck, you duck. When I say stay back, you stay back. And whether I say it or not, you'll stay quiet and stay out of the way." His warm cinnamon gaze turned to cold quartz crystal and held hers. "If there's trouble, you run. I'll worry about Zak and Nate."

"Who will worry about you?"

"Nobody needs to worry about me."

The way he looked just then, a rock of determination and strength, she could almost believe him.

"So take whatever last chance we have here to rest. We'll both need all our focus and strength," he told her, his voice softening with patience.

She took off her coat. He ordered food. They ate. She didn't taste any of it. Five minutes later, she couldn't have said for a million dollars what the toppings on the pizza had been. The air was filled with tension. Her accusations of him, her blaming him for what had happened were part of that. She knew she wasn't being entirely reasonable, but she was too petrified for her babies, too emotionally wrung out to take the words back.

All she could do was stare out the window at the cops who were milling around the house. Were they still hoping to find some clues out there, or were they here for protection? She asked Reid.

He shrugged. "Both, I'm guessing."

He kept checking his e-mail. Nothing was coming

in. He paced the room for hours on end. When darkness fell, he ordered food again. The cops left, but an unmarked police car with two plainclothes officers was now parked in front of the house.

Every time Reid's phone rang, she jumped. But it was never a call that brought any answers.

"The kidnappers didn't say when they were calling back?" she asked for at least the third time.

He shook his head. "Go to bed. Get some rest."

"I can't." She kept staring out the window at a row of streetlights, hoping that somehow, by some miracle, she would see her babies being brought back.

She chewed every nail she had down to bloody stumps, and she'd never chewed her nails in her life. She was ready to start pulling her hair out by the time midnight rolled around and Reid's phone rang again.

He picked up and listened for ten or fifteen minutes with only the occasional, brief question. "Okay. Thanks." He hung up, then looked at a picture of a man on the phone's display. "They might have found the virus."

She'd been hoping for, *we have the babies,* but this was something. At least they were heading in the right direction. "Where?"

"At a fertility clinic not far from here. A friend of a friend knows a guy, Jason Wurst, who's sold something like this abroad before to supplement his research grant. Couldn't pin it on him at the time, but the man who investigated the case swears by it."

She stared. "An ob-gyn?" What did that have to do with deadly viruses?

"Not exactly. A hard of his luck scientist who helps out at the clinic so he has access to the cryogenic freezer. His ex-wife worked on the original project for the government. She died of unknown causes a few months after the project was closed. I'm guessing our Jason here blames the government, whether or not her death was related."

"You think the wife told him about the project? Wouldn't that be confidential?"

"She might have found talking about it irresistible. They were both top scientists at one time. Or she, too, might have blamed the government for falling sick and told her husband in some last, desperate act before her death."

"So he figured out how to make the virus and whipped up a batch. Do you think he still has it with him?"

"Unless our bad guys have a cryogenic freezer at home next to their beer coolers, they wouldn't pick the virus up until the last second, when they're ready to distribute it."

She was on her way to the door. Reid cut in front of her, made sure it was safe to leave before they went to the car, nodding to the cops who were still outside.

"It'd be better if you stayed here with them." He made a last-ditch effort, not looking too surprised when she took the passenger seat without bothering to answer.

One of the cops ran over.

"I'm taking her to another, more secure location,"

Reid told him. "Looks like you're done here. Thanks, guys."

For a while, he drove in silence. And she worked herself into a frenzy of worry. Because so many things could go wrong here.

She wished the kidnappers would call back already. She couldn't stand not knowing what was happening with the boys. She was gripping the laptop hard enough to make the plastic creak, so she peeled her fingers off and wrapped her arms around herself.

"Why me?" Reid asked out of the blue.

A few seconds passed before she could pull her thoughts away from her worries and focus on him. "You what?"

"You obviously don't sleep around. So, two years ago in Hopeville, why did you choose me?"

Chapter Six

Not a question Lara wanted to address in any great detail. Or at all. For, say, the next hundred years. "I'm fine. You don't need to distract me."

"You're not fine. And I want an answer."

Great. How was she supposed to explain?

"You were my first flight lesson," she said at last, after she'd managed to pull her thoughts together.

"Your what?"

She drew a slow, deep breath. "My grandmother, Granny Jordan," she clarified, "was a member of the Ninety-nines. Not a founding member. I mean later."

"A sports team?" he guessed, looking puzzled.

"An organization of women pilots founded by Amelia Earhart."

"You're kidding."

"She was brave and wild and had a life fit for the movies. My mom didn't like her. Probably because my father idolized her. Mom didn't get the whole flying high on the wings of freedom concept."

"But your grandmother was your hero."

"Right. So Dad died when I was twelve, same year

as Granny Jordan, and Mom had even more rules after that. I think she was scared of raising a teenage girl alone. It was like living in a nunnery. Then I went away to college and saw a little freedom for like five minutes before she got sick and I went home to take care of her. Then she died, and I was in a daze for a while. Then my uncle retired to Florida and gave me his butcher shop in Hopeville."

"Why you?"

"He doesn't have any kids. He's too old to do the work. He said he didn't mind if I sold it, but he didn't have the heart to. And I wanted to do that, but then I came to Hopeville, and… Even the name. It had *starting over* written all over it. It was scary. It was something my mother would have never done, and Granny Jordan would have taken on in the blink of an eye."

He nodded. "So where do I come into the picture?"

"I was going to live a life of excitement like my grandmother. You were my first wild adventure." She bit her lip. "And then I learned my lesson."

He gave her a thoughtful look. "I don't think an adventuring spirit can be silenced that easily."

Oh, yes it can. "Mine was," she said to make sure he understood. "Silenced. Dead and buried."

He shook his head. "Is that why, instead of staying at a safe house under protection, you insisted on coming with me to steal a deadly virus from a bunch of terrorists?" For a second, he took his eyes off the road to look at her.

And what she saw in his gaze confused her. There

was warmth there and appreciation and, for a second, a distinct flair of desire.

She swallowed hard and looked away, out the side window at the houses flying by them.

"What if you were born to be wild?" he asked, his voice like a warm, gooey cinnamon roll all of a sudden.

She remembered that voice. It had been her undoing two years ago. She'd had no defenses against it then. She better damn well find some now. And fast.

What did he know about her, anyway?

She was not born to be wild. She wasn't even attracted to wild. She might have been at one point. But definitely not anymore. Life had cured her of that. She was going with Reid simply because she couldn't stand staying behind. She needed to be part of the effort to find her babies.

"Remind me again why the FBI can't go and investigate that virus and this Jason guy?" she asked.

"We don't have the CD the kidnappers want. We'll need something else to negotiate with."

"Is this where the virus comes in?"

"Partially. The virus comes in on many levels. For one, we want to take it out of circulation as soon as possible."

That was good. Made sense. And she was also glad that whoever had taken her babies wanted to negotiate. There was hope then. And Reid was on her side. As much as she hated the idea of who he was, some undercover agent who made a living by spying and fighting, she did appreciate that she had a warrior on her side just now.

When she'd first spotted him at the restaurant, it was as if her most impossible dreams had come true. She could barely believe her eyes. She couldn't have been happier. Then she'd realized that he wasn't the man she'd thought he was. That all he'd ever done was lie to her. That she hadn't meant anything to him, as proven by the fact that he could leave her without a second thought. And then she got mad. Disappointed and hurt, too, but mostly angry as hell.

Now she was just desperate. She was ready to forgive him for abandoning her if he helped her get Zak and Nate back.

The miles whizzed by them. Interminable minutes followed one another.

"They really are yours, you know," she told him as he took the next exit off the highway and went in the drive-through of a fast-food restaurant. "The boys." She wasn't sure why it was important to make him believe—whether it was so he wouldn't think she was a liar, or maybe some part of her thought that if he truly believed her he would fight harder for them. She didn't examine her motives too closely.

"I know."

Good. So he hadn't changed his mind about that yet again. "How?" she asked.

"I looked into their faces. Burgers okay?"

"Fine. With lots of coffee." She wasn't hungry, but she understood that to keep their strength up they needed to eat at regular intervals. "Everyone says the twins look like me."

"Maybe around the mouth. But my mother could show you some of my baby pictures..." He grinned as he shook his head.

"You have a mother?"

He gave a low grunt. "Are insults really necessary at this stage?" He took their food and got back on the road.

She flashed him a look. "Back when we met, you told me you didn't have a family."

"Right. I try to keep her out of my undercover work." He started on his food.

She started on hers. "Your father?"

"Died in the First Gulf War. He was the same age I am now. We don't know the circumstances."

She stared at him. "What do you mean you don't know?"

"He was MIA for a long time. We kept hoping the Iraqis had him. POW. At least he would have been alive. I was eighteen when he went missing, college freshman. As I said, we kept hoping. The last of the troops came home. July 31, 1991. He didn't come with them. When the second war came around, I looked for him personally. I was in the army by then."

"I'm sorry about your dad," she said, but soon her thoughts went in another direction.

He was watching her. "What? You have that look on your face."

"Zak and Nate have a grandmother." She couldn't

help a small smile. "I always thought they were going to grow up without a father. Always wished that at least they had grandparents. I was always worried that they had nobody but me. What if something happened to me, you know? My uncle is great, but he's pretty far away. And he has too many health issues to take on two little kids if I was no longer in the picture." She shrugged. "Once you become a mother, worries come out of the woodwork to keep you up all night."

"Nothing's going to happen to you," he said brusquely. "And when my mother spoils them rotten, you might wish she lived in Florida."

"Where does she live?"

He hesitated.

Was he, even now, unsure how far he was going to let her and the twins into his life?

But then he said, "Easton."

And she forgot everything else. "That's not far from Hopeville!" A picture flashed in her mind: herself, the boys, Reid, a smiley grandmother.

She mercilessly squashed the image and the feelings it brought. No sense setting herself up for heartache. She had plenty of hurt on her plate at the moment. She wasn't looking for extra servings.

When his phone rang, the food got stuck in her throat. She swallowed painfully as she listened.

"Okay," he was saying. "We can be there in twenty minutes."

"What is it?"

"The exchange is set at an abandoned gas station

sixty miles north of here." He was already executing a U-turn, tires squealing, traffic rules be damned.

Panic squeezed her throat. "But we don't have anything to trade."

"Look in the glove compartment."

She did.

"Pick a CD."

She did. The cover sported lots of chains, leather and makeup—a popular heavy metal band.

"Take out the paper cover. Turn the disc blank side up."

Her hands were shaking all of a sudden, but she managed. "They're going to know."

"Eventually. But we can fool them long enough to get close to the babies and grab them."

Oh, God. She was beginning to hyperventilate.

No. She steadied herself. She wasn't going to fall apart. If Reid could hold tough, then so could she. She would do anything for her babies.

She rolled her shoulders the way she'd seen him do it. Practiced deep breathing. Counted the miles.

The abandoned gas station was dark and empty when they pulled in. Reid picked a spot so that the whole area was visible, at the far corner of the lot where nobody could park behind them. He laid his gun on his lap, pulled his bag of assorted weapons from the backseat and set it at her feet, opened the zipper.

"Can I have one of those?" She held out a hand, hating that her voice was unsteady.

"Are you a good enough shot not to put the babies at risk?"

Her shoulders slumped as she dropped her hand. She'd never shot a weapon before. But she wanted to do something.

"Biggest help would be if you did what I told you, when I told you. No distractions."

She nodded.

When a car went by on the road, they both tensed. They were outside the limits of whatever town lay up ahead. Traffic was sparse in the middle of the night. Endless, painful minutes ticked by, one after the other.

Soon they were ten minutes past the agreed handover time. Then half an hour. Nothing happened, nobody came. Cars went by from time to time, but none of them as much as slowed.

When they had sat there for a full hour in vain, Reid swore under his breath, then pulled out.

"Where are you going?"

"They aren't coming."

"You don't know that." She couldn't bear the thought that the handover wasn't happening. She'd been counting on having her babies back in her arms. All this time she'd been telling herself that it would be only a matter of minutes now.

They had to come.

"This was just a test. They wanted to make sure we were still alone, that we didn't call in the law. We have to get to that clinic. Faking it with the disc would have been okay if we had no other choice. But things will go a hell of a lot easier if we have real leverage."

On some level, his words made sense, but she turned and kept the gas station in sight for as long as she could, hoping until the very last second that someone would show up with her babies.

Reid checked the rearview mirror often as he drove, taking sudden turns, doubling back a couple of times.

"Are we being followed?"

"Might have been. Couldn't tell for sure. We're not anymore," he said with confidence.

She was still shaky with anguish when he pulled into the parking lot of a medical complex and parked in front of a squat, white building.

She reached for the door handle.

"Not yet," Reid said.

"What are we waiting for?"

"It's four in the morning. We're waiting for the clinic to open and for our man to come in."

"Can't we just go in and get what we need?" Normally, she was a law-abiding citizen to the extreme. But there was no line she wasn't willing to cross for Zak and Nate.

"I don't exactly know what the virus would look like. I'm assuming it's a vial among trays and trays of vials. I doubt the bastard has it labeled Deadly Virus. And I need to ask him some questions anyway."

"So we're just going to sit here for hours, waiting?" She couldn't stand the thought of that. By the time the clinic opened, she was going to drive herself crazy with worrying. Every minute that passed, her babies were without her, in danger, possibly getting hurt. The thought was killing her.

"We're going to sleep," Reid said evenly.

"How can you even think of sleeping at a time like this?" Her nerves short-circuited as she hissed the words at him. "Don't you care at all? Don't you know that Zak and Nate are scared right now? Don't you wonder if their diapers have been changed? If they've been fed? Why couldn't we sleep at the gas station, for heaven's sake? We could have given them longer to show up."

He let her smack him in the shoulder. Then he gently took her hands. His gaze held hers. His voice dropped as he said, "They weren't coming. And I care. I can't stand this. But I will, because I have to. I will sleep, because it's the smartest thing to do to keep my body and mind in optimum fighting condition, and I'm planning on fighting to the death if I have to. I will get our boys back." He placed her hands back into her lap. "Now, sleep."

Her skin tingled where he touched her. She tried to rub away the sensation. "I really can't."

He reached over, undid her seat belt and pulled her toward him until her head was resting on his shoulder, his right arm around her. "Try it anyway. I'll leave the motor running for heat."

He laid his head back against his headrest and closed his eyes. His breathing was slowing already.

"I'm sorry I lost it," she said weakly.

"Don't worry about it. You deal with this whatever way you can."

A moment of silence passed between them.

She shifted into a more comfortable position. "Do you do this often? Stakeout, I mean. How do you stand it?"

"When you're undercover, that's how it goes. You spend ninety-nine percent of your time waiting for something to happen that you can either report back or act on."

"What happens with the other one percent?"

"Manure hits the fan, and you wish like hell you were still waiting."

She thought about that, about what his day-to-day life must be like. She had trouble even imagining it. She didn't fight it when, after a while, comforted by his warm body, she felt herself drift off to sleep.

She was awakened by a kiss to her forehead. "Time to roll, sleeping beauty." His voice was rusty, as if he'd just woken up a moment ago.

Dawn was lighting up the sky behind the clinic buildings. Men and women were filtering through the revolving doors at the main entrance.

She pulled away from Reid, ran her fingers through her hair, then her gaze focused on the cold coffee in the cup holder. She drank it to the last drop, startled when Reid suddenly lifted his head and shot out of the car, barking a low, "Stay," as he went

A scrawny, bald guy was getting out of his car one row ahead of them, midfifties, glasses, long gray coat.

Reid maneuvered to get there just as the man put his steaming travel mug on the car's roof and bent to lock the door.

Lara slid out of the car quietly, and moved closer as Reid trapped the guy against his own vehicle.

"Jason?"

"Who are you?" The man scrambled to the side, but couldn't get away once Reid had him by the elbow. "What do you want?" He pulled his neck in.

"I'm here early for the pickup."

Jason's eyes darted from side to side behind his wire-rim glasses. "I don't know what you're talking about."

"I think you do. Let's see what goodies you keep in your freezer." Reid opened his coat and flashed the gun tucked into his waistband.

Jason turned a shade paler. Reid let his coat drop closed before pushing the man toward the building. He went, but not without argument.

"You can't do this. There are security cameras here." His gaze was darting around, but the parking lot was fairly empty since it was still early in the morning. No one to help him.

Reid patted his coat. "One wrong move and you'll be dead by the time whoever is watching the cameras in the security office gets out here." He spoke matter-of-factly, almost as if bored that he had to explain something so obvious. Yet an underlying menace was present, made even colder by the fact that his words had been spoken so low key.

This is who he is, she thought as a shiver ran across her skin.

He dominated any environment he was in. He was always scanning his surroundings, alert. She didn't think a mouse could have crossed the parking lot without him noticing. The gap between reality and the fantasy man she'd made of him in her mind over the last two years was enormous. And she still grieved for that fantasy man. But she was glad that the real Reid Graham was who he was, here right now and fighting on her side.

The warmth and pull she felt toward him suddenly caught her off guard. His show of strength and that macho alpha-male stuff were kick-starting her hormones. She bit her bottom lip. *No.* Absolutely not. Sure, he was still gorgeous. Sure, he had a body to make her go cross-eyed just being next to him. But she wasn't going to make the same mistake again. She'd grown up a lot since lust for him had so thoroughly turned her head. This time, she so wasn't going to go there.

Would she let him help her get the twins back? Yes. But right after that, they were going their separate ways again.

When some people came toward them, Reid let Jason go. "I'm a very good shot. I wouldn't try anything stupid if I were you."

And even if Jason was completely immoral, he wasn't stupid, apparently, because he kept going without raising a fuss, simply nodding to his colleagues. If they noticed the miserable look on his face, they didn't comment.

"You stay in the waiting area," Reid told her as they

walked into the spacious lobby with its cheerful colors. He hadn't looked back at her since he'd left her in the car but, of course, he would know that she was there, a few steps behind him.

She took one look at the blue plastic chairs by the wall and followed him straight to the back, where Jason opened a door marked Staff Only with his ID card.

The lights were on, which meant there were already some people inside, although they couldn't see anyone as Jason led them to the labs in back. Lara walked in after them, ignoring the deadly glare Reid flashed her.

"I'll need a cooler," he told the man.

Jason pulled one from under a stainless steel desk.

"How long is the virus viable after it's thawed?"

The man shrugged, wouldn't look at them.

Reid went for his gun, lifted the barrel to the guy's forehead. "You want to answer that." His voice was cold enough to compete with the cryogenic freezer.

"Forty-eight hours or more." Jason was cross-eyed looking at the barrel, pulling as far back as the equipment allowed. "But it'll get less potent as time goes on." His voice was as weak as his knees, which were visibly shaking.

His undisguised fear didn't soften Reid. "When is the original pickup scheduled?"

"Friday. Please, don't shoot me. Please."

Christmas Eve?

Lara had to think what day it was now. The last couple of days melted into one. *Monday.* It was Monday. Allen picking her up for their date at her house Saturday night seemed a lifetime ago. She'd never been apart from the twins this long before. She blinked hard, feeling like her heart was breaking in two every time she thought of her little boys.

"Do you have any more of this?" Reid asked after Jason had put on protective gear to spare his hands, and the vials were transferred, the cooler sealed.

Reid was the calmest person in the room. Even Jason's hands shook a little as he moved the virus. She was ready to pass out, frankly. Reid kept up that detached, *been here done this before* attitude. From what she'd seen so far, she didn't think much could shake him.

"Is this all?" he asked Jason again, his voice sharper this time and filled with warning.

The man's shoulders shrunk. "I don't even have the full order. One batch spoiled. Not my fault. I mean, the conditions here—"

"So what does this thing do exactly?"

The guy's face lit up suddenly. "Gradual muscle paralysis. Death by suffocation. Eventually the lungs can't expand enough to allow the infected test subjects to breathe. Well, theoretically. In rats," he added. "The virus isn't viable for long outside the body, but it makes up for that by having a long incubation time. People can pass it on to hundreds of others before they realize that they're infected." He actually sounded proud as he said that, his back straightening.

Then he sobered, his tone urgent as he asked, "What are you going to do with this? I only made it because I had assurance that it would be used *over there*. The people I made it for are sick of our government always pulling its punches. Take this over and bring our boys home. I'm a patriot."

And she could tell from the sudden fire in the man's eyes that he did believe that. He didn't resent the government for his wife's death. He probably thought of his wife as a heroic casualty in a war that wasn't going too far. So he'd decided to take up the banner.

Reid looked like he was about to pistol-whip him, but a ring tone interrupted. When he pulled the phone from his pocket, she saw it was Kenny's, not his.

Kenny's phone. Which meant this was a call from whoever had taken Zak and Nate. She stepped closer to Reid. They had to be calling with another time and location for the exchange. And now she and Reid had something real to trade, something important the kidnappers wouldn't want to mess with.

Every muscle in her body went rigid as she waited, hoping with all she was that she would get her babies back this time. She didn't think she could make it without them for another day.

She and Reid were close now, she told herself. They had the virus. The virus was the key. Reid would make the exchange. All they had to do in the meantime was make sure that nothing bad happened to that cooler and they didn't end up infecting themselves and half the state.

Chapter Seven

"Where the hell were you?"

"We'll meet tonight."

"No," Reid said into the phone. "Let's not drag this out. I'm ready now."

Lara gripped his hand and squeezed. After experiencing little but her anger and disapproval for the past two days, the gesture warmed something inside him—even as mad as he was at her for having followed him into the clinic.

She was looking up at him, her violet eyes full of questions, but hope, too. She trusted him to save their children. Trusted him when she had little reason to, based on their past. He wasn't going to fail her this time. He wasn't going to fail his sons.

"Tonight. Five minutes to midnight. Down by the river at the foot of the old railroad bridge, like I said." The line went dead with the last word.

He could have smashed Kenny's phone against the wall, or against Jason's head.

"They'll kill me for this," the man muttered, stealing

a step back. "You don't know who you're messing with. They'll kill all three of us."

"You deserve to die. Me and her?" He glanced at Lara, no longer surprised by the wave of tender, protective feelings running through him. "I'd like to see them try."

He strode out of the lab, through the office, nodding to a nurse behind the single occupied workstation. The key was to act as if he belonged here. Everyone else must still be in the lunchroom, having their morning coffee, gossiping, fortifying themselves for the day.

"What did they say?" Lara wanted to know as soon as they were outside and had a private moment. She was hanging on to his free hand.

He had to pull away. For one, he didn't want to give her the false impression that they were now a team. Two, he needed a free hand so he could go for his gun if something unexpected happened.

She didn't miss the gesture. Folded her arms in front of herself. "What did they say?"

He wished he could give her better news. He slowed a little so he could look at her fully. "Handover is at five minutes to midnight."

"That's almost a whole day." Her lower lip trembled once before she flattened her mouth, visibly gaining control of her emotions.

She was good at that. Always pulling it together. He supposed she couldn't afford to fall apart. She was a business owner, a single mother raising twins. All alone. He clenched his jaw.

"What are they waiting for?" she asked.

"Could be they need that long to secure the location. Could be they're messing with us. Or maybe they just want the cover of darkness." He settled the cooler carefully on the backseat, then got in. And couldn't not think of the hundred things that could have gone wrong in the last fifteen minutes. He shot her a cold glare. "Next time I say stay in the car, you stay."

"You could have needed backup."

He didn't need backup. On principle. "I work *alone*." He emphasized the last word.

She had that offended look on her face. She still wasn't getting it. As if to prove that, she said, "What if he had a gun?"

"Exactly." He pinned her with a sharp look. "What if he had a gun? What if he dropped a vial on purpose? Don't you want to be around to raise those kids?"

She went so pale, he almost regretted that last bit. But he had to make her understand. "Next time I say you stay, you stay."

She nodded slowly.

And when they got back on the road, for a long time neither of them spoke.

"What about Jason?" she asked at last. "Shouldn't you have apprehended him or whatever it is people like you do?"

People like him? "I don't think he would have come with us willingly and quietly. I could have grabbed him and dragged him out of there at gunpoint. Some do-gooder would have called the cops." They sure didn't need that. He weighed his next words. "I'm not exactly operating on the books here."

She turned to face him, her violet eyes narrowing. "What are you talking about?"

"I'm supposed to have you holed up in a safe place, making sure you're nice and comfortable while we wait. The powers that be weren't overjoyed with my personal connection to all this."

Her eyes went wide. "They took you off the case?" She blinked. "You're not even supposed to be here doing this?" She looked like she was trying to decide whether to cry or strangle him to death.

Since she wasn't the weepy kind, things didn't look good for him.

"Hey. Take it easy. We're doing pretty good so far, aren't we? And," he felt the need to point out, "if I was conducting this as an official operation, I couldn't be dragging a civilian along, could I? You'd be sitting in some safe house, cooling your heels." Come to think of it, he should have gone for that option. But he'd fallen for those violet eyes and let her tag along despite his better judgment. What the hell was wrong with him?

Her shoulders relaxed a little. She leaned back in her seat. "Might as well be at the safe house. We're doing nothing but waiting."

She was right, but there was nothing to do about that waiting. The best he could do was make sure that when the time for the handover came, he was ready. He pulled his own phone from his pocket.

"I need a couple of favors," he said when the other

end was picked up. He was going to catch hell when this was all over. He might as well go all the way.

"Am I going to have to court-martial you for them?" his superior officer, Colonel Wilson, asked on the other end.

"Probably."

The colonel huffed. "I hear congratulations are in order."

"Carly has a big mouth."

"She meant well. She gave me the heads-up so I had some inkling in case you needed help. I was calling her for a consult on something else."

"I need a pickup for some serious virus. Should be kept in a cryogenic freezer. I need identical vials with tap water. I need someone to pick up Jason Wurst, the guy I got the virus from." He gave the code of the GPS tracker he'd stuck on Jason's car when he'd hauled him out of the driver's seat. "And I need another car. Bulletproof would be good."

"I need you to stop engaging in illegal activities that break the chain of command, will get the FBI breathing brimstone and fire down my neck and jeopardize our core mission. Coming in for a complete debriefing would be a good start."

"Yes, sir. Soon. I swear."

A few seconds of silence passed. "Twin boys, huh?"

"Zak and Nate."

"Let's hope they look like their mother."

"Very funny, sir." He relaxed a little at the colonel's lighter tone.

His relief proved to be premature, however. The next thing the man said was spoken in a hard, crisp voice. "I officially, and in every other capacity, reject your request, soldier. This is an FBI operation. I shouldn't have to remind you that you're off the case. As of now, you're under direct order from me to stop all activities relating to this case and hand over the virus, as well as all information in your possession, to your FBI handler. And if your buddy Cade, who is sitting in my office and heard most everything, gets it in his thick head that he should help you, meeting up with you at some undisclosed location like his hunting cabin to provide you with all you requested, you two will be facing court-martial together. Is that understood?"

"Yes, sir." He pulled onto Route 1 as the colonel hung up.

"Where are we going?"

"To meet a friend."

He was grateful for the colonel's help, even if the man couldn't spell it out over the phone. He could only hint at hooking him up with Cade.

In an hour, they were up by Levitt Hill where Cade Palmer, an old SDDU buddy of his, had bought a hunting camp not long ago. Reid had been at the initiation party during the last hunting season, with some of the others from the team. Since they were all crack shots, and didn't consider hunting with a gun much of a challenge, they'd gone out with bows and arrows. And still ended up donating a load of venison to homeless shelters all around the area. None of the married guys had been allowed to take Bambi home.

He glanced at Lara. If they'd been together at the time, not only would she have been happy to see his ten-point buck, she would have gutted, skinned and chopped it all up for him. She was a helluva woman by his standards. Had never known better. Next hunting season, Cade and the rest of the guys could eat their hearts out.

The realization of what he was thinking brought him up short. She wouldn't be with him next fall. The thought was a direct hit, ripping a hole in his chest. *Dammit.*

Not that he didn't deserve some pain. Even before the current danger he was dragging her into, he'd hurt her in the past, without meaning to, without realizing how much he'd hurt her.

"Back in Hopeville, two years ago—" he began, having no idea how he was going to finish. He wasn't one for sharing his feelings. Hell, he wasn't one for *having* feelings. He would have just as soon gone on a minesweeping mission as have a heart-to-heart with a woman. But Lara deserved the truth from him. "I wasn't just passing time with you. I meant everything." Okay. There it was. *Do with that what you will.*

She gave him a stunned look, then shook her head. "I can't deal with all that now. Let's get the twins back first. Then we can talk about the rest."

Thank God above. She didn't want to talk. "Fair

enough," he said quickly before she could change her mind. You never knew with a woman.

But when she did talk, she seemed to have a completely different topic on her mind. "How did you learn to bake?" she asked after a few minutes. Probably to distract herself, or maybe because she, too, had been thinking about that brief week they'd spent together two years ago.

They had time and she needed a distraction, so he decided to tell her, although he couldn't remember the last time he'd shared anything personal about his past with anyone, not even his SDDU buddies.

"My grandfather was an old-fashioned English country baker. I was pretty young when he died. To keep his memory alive, my mom and I baked one of his recipes every Sunday. I thought that was the height of indignity for a boy. I would have rather been playing ball with my friends outside. But she was so broken up. I faked it for her at the beginning, then the thing grew on me.

"In high school, I got a job at the local bakery to save up for college. When I got kicked out of Penn State for fighting and went into the army, I enlisted as a cook. Then I left the army and did other things." He left that topic alone. "Anyway, when I had to go undercover in Hopeville, we looked at a couple of covers. There was the empty bakery right in the same strip mall where Jimmy had his gun shop. Seemed like a good fit. Perfect to keep an eye on him and whoever was coming and going."

"You know that crusty roll recipe you showed me?" she asked quietly.

He nodded.

"I still make it."

Something turned over in his chest, the same funny feeling he'd had when she'd told him that she still visited his grave. The pull he felt toward her, both physical and emotional, was getting more and more difficult to resist. Good thing he'd made up his mind early on that nothing was going to happen between them this time. What he could give her—precious little—was not what she needed. He'd broken the rules with her once. To break them again would be unforgivably selfish.

"So tell me about this boyfriend of yours. Allen," he said, then winced when her eyes grew somber.

"Do you think he's okay?" She bit her lower lip. "If anything happens to him… He has nothing to do with anything. I couldn't forgive myself if—" She swallowed hard and looked away.

Damn. With everything that was going on, he'd forgotten to tell her the news.

"He's fine. I got a call just before I came back to the safe house and found the boys gone and Ben shot. I forgot to tell you. Sorry." He rolled his shoulders. "So this guy, he matters to you?"

"He's okay? Oh, thank God." She slumped back, squeezing her eyes shut for a second, drawing a deep breath. "He's nice. We were just getting to know each other."

He wasn't sure how he would have felt if she'd said

she was in love with the man. When he tried to picture Allen by her side, as her lover, as stepfather to the twins, the hot rage that flooded through him left him unbalanced.

"Well, he's right as rain," he said. She needed to hear something positive, even if he wasn't nearly as relieved by the news as she seemed to be.

She was lost in her thoughts for the rest of the ride, and he let her be, most topics of conversation suddenly seeming a minefield between them. Once they got to the cabin, he left her in the car while he walked the cooler over to a waiting Hummer.

"I appreciate this," he told Cade as they made the exchange.

"You better. I don't risk court-martial for just anyone."

"You're not risking it for me either. You're retired from the team."

"True." Cade grinned. "Cabin is open. Use it if you need a rest before you move on. There's a car for you a hundred feet or so up the north trail. Tank filled. Couldn't get bulletproof on this short notice."

"That's fine. Thanks, man."

"Don't mention it. Seriously. Bailey would skin me if she knew that I'm back dabbling in the business. She still hasn't forgiven me for the hunting trip. She's trying to talk me into doing catch-and-release next year."

He took a second to sort that out. "Like what? Give first aid to the deer? Catch-and-release only works for fish."

"Women. They are a mystery." Cade rolled his eyes good-naturedly.

He couldn't agree more. But although the guys always played the tough macho male in front of each other, Reid could see the undisguised love in his friend's eyes. A look that said not only would he be willing to give up hunting for the woman he loved, he would gladly give up breathing, laying down his life for her if there was a need.

"You helping me out doesn't mean you're back in the business. It's a one-time deal," Reid told him. Theirs was a dangerous occupation, and he had no intention of dragging Cade back into it.

"Damn straight. Pregnancy hormones are scary. I tell you, that kid cannot come out fast enough."

Reid glanced toward his car where Lara sat, her head leaning against the headrest, her eyes closed. He'd missed the whole pregnancy thing with her.

Well, that was an enormous relief. He didn't understand where that heavy feeling in his chest had come from.

"Although, when you consider what a miracle it is, everything else seems like a small price to pay," Cade added.

"I'm only personally involved as long as it takes to get the boys back. After that, it'll be a long-distance thing. I wouldn't be good for them. The best thing for everyone is if we go our separate ways."

Cade flashed him a doubtful look, but didn't say anything.

IF SHE THOUGHT they were going to spend the day sitting around, she was mistaken. Reid had the cabin transformed into command headquarters in no time. Calls were coming in from his friends one after the other.

Jason had been picked up. Apparently, the FBI had been tipped off to his little arrangement at the clinic and was out there right now collecting evidence. Carly was calling in with explanations on every new file she cracked on the CD. Another friend was apparently driving by that railroad bridge in question and sending in photos. There were even aerial photos from some satellite. Reid had grinned pretty wide when he'd gotten that one, and muttered something like, "Thank you, Colonel."

In between fielding calls, he was going over his maps. Over and over. And checking his weapons.

"I want one," she said at last, coming to a decision. "I want you to teach me how to use it."

He looked up from his work. "Are you sure?"

She expected some resistance. His immediate agreement, his faith in her, was gratifying. Yet she felt wary of it. She didn't want to like him. He was the reason why she was in this mess, the reason her babies were in danger. But it was becoming more and more difficult to maintain that edge of anger toward Reid when she saw how hard he was working to get Zak and Nate back.

And yet, she had to keep the wall up. So maybe she could forgive him—he hadn't meant for any of this to happen. But she couldn't go beyond that. No liking him, no needing him. Definitely no wanting him. He would leave as soon as she had the twins back. He'd been clear about that. And, of course, that was exactly what she wanted. Definitely.

Who needed all this danger, upheaval and excitement? Not her. She craved safe and steady.

He pulled a small handgun from his bag. "All right. Watch this. This is how you load it." He popped bullets into the magazine. "This is how you take off the safety."

Didn't look too complicated. And just because she wanted to learn how to use a gun, since she might need that skill in the very near future, didn't mean that she was getting drawn into his kind of life.

He handed her the loaded gun and stood. "Let's see if you can hit anything."

They went behind the cabin. He picked up a stone and put it on top of a woodpile. Then he came and stood next to her as she lifted the weapon.

"Line up the sight. Lock your knees, lock your elbows. Don't wait too long. The longer you wait, the more your arms will shake. Lift, aim, shoot."

She lowered her arms, then lifted the gun again, looked at the stone and imagined the masked man who'd grabbed her babies while the other was tying her up. She squeezed the trigger. The stone flew up in the air.

Reid capped her on the shoulder. "Pretty impressive. You're a natural." He grinned at her with genuine admiration.

She grinned back, feeling better, feeling as if she might have some sort of control for the first time. She could and would fight for her sons. She was pretty sure Reid wouldn't ask her to stay behind this time.

She liked the small surge of confidence that came from her newfound competency. Although, part of her wouldn't have minded some learning curve. He didn't even have a chance to put his arms around her to show how to properly line up the sight.

Surprise at the thought made her blink hard. Since when had she wanted Reid Graham to put his arms around her? "I better shoot a few more rounds," she said to yank her thoughts back from that track.

He lined up a dozen stones this time.

She missed the first, got the next four right, missed another one, then finished the row.

"You have seriously good aim."

"Exactly why I still have ten fingers. You can't have bad aim and wield a cleaver for a living."

"I didn't think about that," he admitted, then smiled even wider, revealing strong, white teeth. "Hand-eye coordination is a beautiful thing." He lifted a hand and brushed his thumb across her jaw.

Their gazes locked. She couldn't move as he lowered his head to hers.

"And so is lip-to-lip coordination," he said before he kissed her. Deeply. With military thoroughness.

Her brain was as foggy as a Scottish Highland meadow on a cold fall morning. "Oh," she stammered when he pulled away. "But why?"

"You don't know what it does to a guy when he sees a hot woman shoot like Dirty Harry."

The only word that registered with her was *dirty.*

She drew a shaky breath, gathered her thoughts. Okay, so there was some leftover attraction, but they didn't need to act on it. Falling back in lust with him again would be the stupidest thing she could do.

"Pretty reckless, aren't you?" She shot a pointed glance at the gun in her hand. "What if I didn't like it?"

"I counted the bullets, just in case," he said.

And kissed her again.

Damn the man, he had an answer for everything.

SHE'D LET HIM KISS HER. More than once, so neither could claim that it had been an accident. Damn if he knew what that meant.

What the hell was wrong with him? Why did he have to kiss her?

Lara had asked him that same question, more politely worded. Reid had given her a glib answer, one that disguised how much the kiss had shaken him. He'd written off that one runaway kiss at the safe house to surprise. After Hopeville, he hadn't expected to ever see her again. She'd taken him off guard by being even more beautiful than he remembered, having turned into an amazing woman.

One small judgment error. That was supposed to be the end of it.

He wasn't supposed to be kissing her again. He was going to walk away when this was over. He tried to remind himself of that as he went through the latest file Carly had sent him, while Lara warmed up the food Cade had left for them.

"You have some pretty good friends. Part of your team?"

"We don't really work as a team." SDDU soldiers mostly worked lone-wolf operations. All information on missions was disseminated on a need-to-know basis. He didn't even know all the team members, aside from the ones he'd met in training, or at the colonel's office, or on the rare joint mission.

Yet, he had to admit, Cade and Carly had come through for him. Long-held beliefs were reorganizing themselves in his head. Lara and the kids were making him look at things in a new way. He'd always thought of himself as a lone soldier, which worked for him just fine. He preferred things that way.

But Lara was right. The SDDU was more than a unit of independently operating commando guys who went on undercover missions all over the world. There *was* something that held them all together. A link that was much stronger than he'd realized.

He hated links. Links were a good way to hurt someone or get yourself hurt, messing up some critical mission. Soldiers like him ought to be able to stand on their own two feet. Except that he *had* reached out this time. And aid had been given to him unconditionally. And it had really helped. At the moment, having Cade and Carly and even Lara on his side, he felt stronger, not weaker.

"Reid?"

He looked up from the laptop, stashing away that last thought.

"I appreciate you helping me."

"They're my boys, too." And, man, was that weird to say. "But I'd help even if they weren't."

"We'll get them back tonight, right? And then this will be all over and everything will go back to the way it was before." She was slightly bent forward over the stove, a few curls of her silky hair falling in front of her face, her amazing body outlined by the firelight.

The way it was before... She and the boys in Hopeville. He in a fake life somewhere far away from her, deep undercover. Damned if that picture didn't burn his stomach like acid. But he said, "Sure, honey."

She smiled at him, a smile that warmed his heart. "We make a good team, don't we?" There was something in her eyes....

He knew without a doubt that danger lay that way for the both of them. They couldn't fall back into some sentimental memory. They couldn't pretend that if they gave into temptation, it would lead somewhere this time.

"What we have here..." He paused. "Don't overestimate it, okay?" A warning that he should heed himself. "To get those boys back, you would have teamed up with the devil." He was warning her off, even as he wanted nothing more than a kiss.

She looked at him for a good, long time, understanding what he was saying, the smile slipping off her face, a thoughtful look replacing it as she whispered, "Maybe I did."

He swore under his breath. The sane part of him knew he needed to keep her at arm's length. The rest of him wanted to gather her in his arms, demanding to know what a few more kisses could hurt. At least he'd have some memories to take with him when the time came to walk away.

Chapter Eight

The woodstove was going full blast in the one-room cabin, thanks to Cade, who had a considerable woodpile out back. A small kitchen took up the front, the same stove used for heating and cooking. One bed was pushed against the back wall. There was enough room in between for the five or six camping beds that she'd seen folded up in a shed out back.

Next to the shed stood an old-fashioned outhouse, which due to winter temperatures was a lot less spider-infested than she had expected. Thank God for small mercies. Blood and gore she was fine with, but bugs seriously scared her, a weakness she covered up in front of the boys as much as she could.

She didn't want Zak and Nate to be afraid of anything. Which meant she would have to set a good example.

And what kind of an example would their father set if he took part in their lives? That was the thought she was chewing over as she headed out to the facilities while it was still light enough outside to see what she was doing. When she was done, she went back in to wash up. A basin of water waited on the kitchen table. She'd already used some of it to wash the dishes.

Reid lay on the bed, fully clothed. "I already washed. That's clean water for you," he said, and turned to the wall.

As if that made her feel more comfortable. She stared at his wide back for a second. To take off her clothes or not, that was the question. His presence was impossible to ignore. The awareness of him in the room sent tingles across her skin.

Stupid, stupid, stupid. They had some leftover chemistry, they made a good temporary team, but what they had was nothing special. He'd all but spelled that out for her. Anger that was becoming familiar filled her little by little. Good. At least that was a safe emotion when she was around him.

She took off her coat. Pulled off her bulky sweater. Hesitated on the long-sleeved T-shirt. Then realized she hadn't had a shower in two days. She yanked the T-shirt off, then her bra, washed as quickly as she could before she dressed again with lightning speed. Then she put the basin on the floor, stripped below the waist and washed the rest of her body, careful not to soak her bandages on her ankles and wrists.

When she was done, she took the water outside, almost dumped it right in front of the door, but realized that it would freeze by morning, so she took it over to the side where nobody would slip on it. When she went back in, she locked the door behind her.

Reid had turned off the generator earlier, but the fire

lit the place sufficiently, so she didn't miss the overhead lights. He still lay with his back to her.

She took a tentative step closer. "Where do I sleep?"

He shifted closer to the wall, leaving a foot-wide space on the bed.

She glanced at the floor. Cold and hard. Then thought of the fold-up beds in the shed. They were freezing cold. And probably the winter residence of all the spiders who'd gone into hiding from the cold weather.

"We'll rest a couple of hours, then get on the road around eleven. That should get us to the bridge in time," he said without turning.

She sat on the side of the bed. The mattress was still warm from his body. She ignored the yearning that unfurled low in her belly. "What if we oversleep?"

"I don't oversleep."

"Would you set an alarm anyway?"

He pulled out his cell phone and did. "Just so you can rest. Stop worrying."

Good advice. If only she could take it. She lay down with her back to him, her feet still on the floor. When she felt comfortable with that, she pulled her feet up. They stayed like that, quiet in the darkness, listening to each other breathing. Then she could feel the mattress shift as he turned onto his back behind her.

"Do you realize that we have two kids together and this is the first time we ever shared the same bed?"

That so did *not* help her relax. "Don't get your hopes up," she said drily.

He gave a low chuckle. "It wasn't my hopes that you used to get up, back in the old days."

She flushed crimson. She was the mother of two. She was a cleaver-wielding, tough-chick butcher, for heaven's sake. She resented the whole pink-cheeked business. Thank God, he couldn't see her face.

"I lusted after you pretty much from the get-go," he admitted with a manly sigh.

And, although her face was still burning, she didn't stop him from saying more.

"I walked over to see who was next door. You had your back to the door, using that industrial meat grinder, wearing that little red apron of yours, cinched around a narrow waist...plenty of curves above and below. Damn." He clicked his tongue. "It was like walking into a fantasy. A centerfold operating heavy machinery."

"Well, if you're going to mock me—"

"You had your hair up, the sun coming in the window, hitting the sweet curve of your neck where a man would give anything to be able to press his lips against. Hell, I was ready to vault over the counter."

"You didn't."

"You turned."

"And I was a disappointment?" She braced for hurt feelings.

"Yes."

She wrapped her arms around herself. What did she care what he'd thought of her anyway?

"Way too young. I told myself I couldn't come anywhere near you." He gave a pained laugh. "We both know how long that lasted. I'm sorry, Lara." He put a warm hand on her arm, just below her shoulder.

"What part did you regret the most, exactly?" she asked, annoyed, because she hadn't regretted any of it.

To give him credit, he actually thought before he gave his answer. "Hard to say. Not the making love part, for sure. And the leaving part couldn't be helped." Then he added in a low voice, "I regret that I wasn't someone else, the kind of guy who could have stayed and deserved you."

That about melted her heart. She had to work hard to get to her anger. "Zak and Nate are not mistakes."

"No." His lips connected with the sensitive skin at her nape as he grazed her skin. "This is where that sunlight danced when I first saw you," he whispered, then dragged his lips over the spot again.

She felt that touch all the way down to her toes. And had to realize that, as much as she'd matured and grown up over the last two years, she was still hopelessly out of her depth with this man, even if he didn't mean anything by what he was doing. At best, he was only trying to comfort her.

"You cut your hair," he said, his warm breath fanning her skin.

Electric currents ran down her spine. "It beats having to pull it up all the time or wearing hairnets."

"I always thought you looked hot in a hairnet."

"You were probably distracted by all that machinery I was operating." A reluctant smile split her lips. "Hairnets don't go with anything."

"Then again, in a sexy hairnet, who needs other clothing?" His voice dropped some, its low tone making her want to melt back into his arms.

Her breath stopped as she caught herself.

Nothing good could come of something like this. Her first instinct was to run. But she had nowhere to go. She had to face him. She turned around slowly, reaching for her anger again, worried that it was becoming more and more difficult to find. "Are you kidding me? We're flirting now? You're coming on to me? Haven't you learned anything?"

"Apparently not." He drew a slow breath that made his wide chest rise in a most distracting way. Then he gathered her closer and kissed her lips.

She was so going to fight him this time. *Tooth and nail.*

She fell into the kiss, into his heat and the comfort his body offered. She submerged herself in the oblivion of it all.

She was going to fight it...soon. Any minute now.

But the kissing went on for a good, long time before she slowly gathered herself. "No way." She pushed him away at last. "This is not going to happen."

"Why?"

"Because I said so." She raised an indignant eyebrow and hoped he wouldn't realize that she was faking all the bluster, that another touch, a single finger caressing her heated skin would likely do her in.

"I liked it better when you were all shy and innocent."

"Is that how you remember me?"

"Yeah." The flames from the stove reflected in his eyes, which looked dark-chocolate in this light. "But mostly, I just remember how hot you were and how hot and bothered you got me. Thank God for that baker's apron. It hid a lot of embarrassing moments, if you know what I mean." He gave a wicked grin.

Her cheeks flared again. At least her face was in the shadows. She needed a second to gather herself. *Don't think tented aprons. Think something responsible. Think family.* "I was never shy. I take after Granny Jordan. I do what I have to. That was her motto."

"The more I hear about her, the more I like her."

That warmed her heart, since Granny Jordan had meant more to her than just about any other person in her family. "I don't know what she would have made of you," she admitted.

"Probably not much." His face clouded over as he looked beyond her toward the fire. "Having done the things I've done. Sometimes you're on a path, and you don't realize how steep it is. Before you know it, you've rolled so damned far, you can no longer even see any other roads you could have taken. There's such a thing as having gone too far for a turnaround."

Something in his voice squeezed her heart and made her want to reach out to him. She didn't. Silence stretched between them.

"You're not what I remembered either," she said at last.

He drew a slow breath and seemed to shake off the moment of melancholy, his lips tugging into a grin. "More handsome and wider in the shoulders?"

She ignored that, biting back a smile. "I had this gentle-giant thing going in my head. Great body, great tattoos, great bike, but a pastry chef at heart."

He gave a deep chuckle. "I wish."

"I never saw you wielding anything more dangerous than a wire whisk." Might as well go for the full, embarrassing truth. "I always thought that had you lived, we would have fallen in love and gotten married, raised the twins together. In my fantasies, you were a doting father."

"You fantasized about me?" Interest gleamed in his eyes.

"No. Just the father part, I mean." She pressed her lips together and cast her gaze down. The dreams she used to have about him… She wouldn't admit to those under torture.

"Uh-huh."

"You know, it's a miracle you, your ego and I can all fit on this bed." She turned her back to him before he could read too much in her face.

He pulled her against him, back to front, and left his arm around her waist. "I fantasized a lot about you," he said into her ear, in that bad-boy voice of his that used to drive her crazy.

Heat gathered instantly at the vee of her thighs. His

hand dipped to her waist. Banked heat flared into flames. He nibbled her neck below her ear. And suddenly it was as if the past two years had never happened.

Warning. Warning. Proceed immediately to the nearest emergency exit, an insistent voice said deep inside, but the rest of her failed to heed the alarm. In her mind, they were back in the bakery again. His scent was the same, the feel of his lips, the way he could unleash a firestorm inside her with a touch. When he gently turned her in his arms, she didn't resist.

"We should be resting," he mumbled against her lips, each word a caress.

"I'm too wired to sleep."

"I could relax you."

He was a cad. Totally incorrigible. But she didn't seem to be able to hate him for that. Where was all that anger when she needed it? When had that seeped away? She felt naked and defenseless without it, even as her body cheered for the possibility of *naked.*

He took her lips, gently but thoroughly, their bodies pressed tightly together. His arousal was unmistakable.

How many times had she dreamed dreams like this? A hundred, two? Only to awaken frustrated in the morning. Frustrated first, then heartbroken because memories of the call from the fire department would come next. The call that had informed her with regret that the two stores had burned. That one body had been found at the bakery.

But she knew now that it hadn't been him. He was

alive—really, really alive—in her arms. And while on a certain level she still felt hurt and resentment over the lies he'd told her, on another level there was nothing but pure relief. Then there was the level of lust. Sheesh, suddenly she had more levels than one of those underground parking garages in the city. And if she were smart, she would listen to that faint voice of sanity in her head and start circling right now for the exit.

Instead, she pressed even closer to him and lost herself in his kiss.

THE SMALL SOUND of capitulation she made in the back of her throat nearly made him lose all control. He was blind with lust and need. But not so far gone that he wouldn't remember who was in his arms and what losing all control could do to her.

Clearly, what he was doing was wrong—no matter how good it felt, no matter what a fantastic memory it would make, just the thing to pull out on a cold, lonely winter night. "I'm sorry, but I'm going to have to stop this," he mumbled against her soft lips. "In a minute."

Another kiss couldn't hurt. It wasn't all just for him. She had to get her mind off their troubles. She needed to relax a little.

Right. A humanitarian mission. His conscience prickled. But the roar of need in his body drowned out every other voice in his brain.

Her long-sleeved cotton shirt sailed over her head before he knew what he was doing. She wore a plain cotton bra, with the barest of lace trim. Whoever had come up with the phrase *plain cotton* obviously hadn't seen this little number.

So much blood was rushing south in his body that he was beginning to feel light-headed. He pressed his face into the soft valley of her breasts, hoping to catch his breath. Except that when he turned his head, through the thin material his lips grazed a nipple accidentally—at least, he thought accidentally—and he lost the ability to breathe altogether.

Then without any planning at all on his part, the nipple was in his mouth, and it was just as sweet as he remembered. Never had he wanted another woman as he wanted Lara Jordan. Not two years ago and not now. And going any further was a bad idea now, just as it had been back then.

Worse.

So he was going to stop. This very second.

His right hand, which went for her other breast, seemed to have missed that briefing.

Okay. Cut to the parting kiss. He moved his head up and claimed her lips. Then she moaned into his mouth, and he forgot that parting kisses were best kept short and sweet.

Who made that rule anyway? If a kiss was all he was going to get, he was going to get his money's worth, a very insistent part of him—not his brain—reasoned. Then, while his lips were busy, his hands used the distraction to get into the action. Next thing he knew, her bra was AWOL. The little tease and his shirt must have run away as a team, because her hard nipples seemed to be pressing against his bare chest in a most enticing way.

He took a split second to look down. Yep. Amazing breasts. Skin to skin.

“Isn’t this a really bad idea?” she asked, looking sweetly dazed.

“We’re adults. In a seminude situation. With full control of it. Hardly a capital offense.”

Then he felt her hands at his belt and he swallowed hard. If those pants came off, Operation Self-Control, well, semi-self-control at this stage, would come to an abrupt end. Unfortunately, every cell in his body clamored toward that goal.

He grabbed her hips and held her still. Put an inch or two distance between their lips. Rested his forehead against hers.

“No.” His voice was so hoarse and full of pain he barely recognized it.

“I don’t want to stop,” she lifted her chin and whispered against his lips.

The exact same words that she’d said two years ago. And he’d been a jerk to give up all common sense and take that for a full green light.

“No,” he repeated this time. “You’re killing me here.”

They lay side by side like that for a long moment, both of them still breathing hard.

Then she went slack and crossed her arms, covering her breasts, turning her head down so she wouldn’t have to look into his eyes. "I'm sorry. Oh, God. I don't know what's gotten into me."

Not him. Unfortunately. "Hey." He turned her and pulled her back against him, and tugged the blanket until it was over them. "There are a lot of high emotions running amok right now. We just slipped for a second here. It won't happen again."

Like hell it won't, his body assured him immediately. He ignored that voice of unbridled need. Of all the women he'd ever known, how unfair was it that he had to be in this situation with Lara? The only one he had a track record of being unable to resist.

"We're older now," she whispered against his chest, her warm breath tickling his skin. "Thank God, we're too smart to make the same mistake."

"Right," he lied through his teeth.

They had three hours before they had to get going. She was lying half-naked in his arms. He could feel her nipples poking against his skin. If he managed to keep his hands off her, it would be a major miracle.

If he had that much gallantry and self-restraint in him, Colonel Wilson should put him up for a medal.

She was pulling her top back on under the blanket. The next time she spoke, her voice was riddled with guilt. "For a moment, I almost forgot…everything. I can't believe that at a time like this, I could—"

She sounded so wretched all of a sudden that it started an ache in his chest, drawing his attention from what other parts of his body were still demanding.

"The last thing you need is a guilt-trip. Listen to me.

I'm a healthy man, you're a healthy woman. We have a history. We're in an emotionally charged situation. A moment of weakness, wanting some comfort where you can find it… It's okay."

She stayed silent for a while before she said with a frustration-filled voice, "What do these people want, anyway? Why are they doing this? The virus and everything?"

"There are always people who are full of hate, no matter what. You do them the slightest wrong, and they'll hate you as long as you live. You don't do anything at all, and they'll make up something just so they can hate you. Hell, they'll hate you even if you try to help them. That's just the way it is."

"That's stupid."

"It is. They operate out of a position of hate and fear. They get into the whole them-versus-us mentality. Happens all over the world."

"So what set this particular group off?"

"They're antigovernment. Not sure how Jimmy Sparks came to join them. I know Kenny Briggs is in because his father and uncle had been executed by lethal injection for first-degree murder. The current governor was a judge at the time. The current mayor of Philadelphia was the prosecuting attorney. They both went on to brilliant political careers. It sticks in Kenny's craw."

The man wasn't the sharpest tool in the cell, but blind with hate and his need for revenge, he was the worst kind of enemy. And Reid had no reason to believe that other members of the cell would be any better. Something to keep in mind as he stepped among them in a couple of hours to bring Zak and Nate home.

This wasn't a group to reason with. It was a group whose sole reason for existence was to kill.

He looked at Lara, outlined in the firelight, and thought of their boys. And knew that whatever happened at that exchange, he would protect what was his.

Chapter Nine

Lara woke with Reid snuggling her from behind, holding her so tight, as though never wanting to let go. She pushed that fancy thought from her groggy mind. He did want to let her go. He *would* let her go. He'd already told her that.

"Is it time?" she asked without turning.

"We have a few more minutes."

She got up anyway as nerves rushed her.

The fire had died down in the stove. The air in the cabin was nippy, but not freezing. The waiting warmth of his body under the blankets pulled her back.

She moved forward, rubbing her hands up and down her arms. "Does your friend keep coffee around here?"

"Above the sink." He got up and tended the fire while she looked for coffee, sugar and two mugs. He used kindling for some quick heat that wouldn't last long, but was enough to warm a little water.

Then they sat at the small table, fingers wrapped around the warm cups. She tried not to look at him. She looked hideous in the morning: hair sticking out in every direction, bleary-eyed. He looked sexy and rumpled, only his gaze sharp and lethal. He could have been on a magazine cover.

When he finished his coffee, he pushed to his feet. They tidied up the place together.

"We'd better get going," he said as he pulled on his coat and took one last look around.

She was already standing by the door. "Ready."

They talked little on their way up the north trail to the car Cade had left, a white GMC Jimmy with four-wheel drive that looked brand-new. She even stayed quiet on the drive out of the woods. Not that her brain was still sleepy, she was more than awake. But all she could think of was her babies, worrying about them was taking up all her energy.

Then she and Reid were flying down the highway, reaching the bridge a little earlier than the appointed time. In the woods, there had still been some snow on the ground, but here, piles of garbage were stuck in the muddy riverbank, the soft wind tossing lonely plastic bags. The place was deserted, the river flowing darkly ahead of them, the noises of the water filling up the night. The old railroad bridge was a dark relic silhouetted against the sky, nothing but a long stretch of rusty metal.

Spooky, she thought, and shivered at the same time, her nerves already raw.

Reid scanned the area, although he probably had every square foot mapped in his head from the materials his friends had sent to the laptop. He was just double-checking things. His efficiency was comforting at a time like this.

"I'm leaving the keys in the ignition. If anything even looks like it might not work out, you slide over behind the wheel and drive away," he told her.

A second passed before the meaning of his words registered.

"Give it up already. You take the macho thing too far," she snapped. "I don't need you to start channeling Rambo here." She didn't want his overprotection. She wanted her babies. "In case it's not clear to you yet, I'll die before I leave this place without Zak and Nate."

ON THE ONE HAND, LARA'S insubordination drove Reid crazy. He was used to military rule, where the superior officer's word was law. On the other hand, he would have said the same thing in her place. He respected her for that.

He scanned the bridge and the woods on the other side of the river again, grateful for the moonlight. He could pick out the glint of a long-range rifle on the bridge. A sniper. A bad one at that, if he let himself be seen that easily. Then he made out the figure of the man, too. *Cade.* Reid nodded in acknowledgment, and Cade did the same in response, then pulled back into the shadows, becoming virtually impossible to detect the next second.

"Cade's here. He'll be securing the area and providing cover if anything goes south. If there's any gunfire, don't shoot at the bridge."

She whipped her head around to look. Her mouth was set tight, her arms wrapped around her torso. She was practically vibrating with nerves. "I don't see anything."

"That's the point. Keep your gun at hand, but out of sight," he told her when two black SUVs pulled up. Since the windows were tinted, he had no idea how many enemies he was facing.

Four got out.

He pushed his door open and stepped outside, leaving the car door open for cover. "Before we do anything, I want to see the children," he said in the way of greeting.

"Do you have the CD?"

"Do you have the kids?"

The men went for their guns, bringing the hardware out into the open. So did he.

Four more bastards got out of another vehicle. And this time, when the doors opened, he could see that there was nobody else in the cars now but the two drivers.

This wasn't an exchange.

The men were here for the CD, all right, but they had no intention of letting him and Lara leave.

"Okay. Let's see if I got what you came for." He stepped toward the back door, opened it and took out a single ampoule from the biohazard cooler, set it on the hood of the car in its protective plastic holder. "Actually, I have something better than the CD."

One of the men was on his cell already. Probably talking to the boss. The others moved forward.

"What the hell is that?" the heftiest of them demanded.

"I think you know. I have the rest, too. Not here, of course. I have your whole order. Jason might be a misunderstood scientific genius, but he's a coward. He wasn't exactly willing to protect the goods with his dead body."

The man on the cell phone was still talking.

Reid pocketed the ampoule. "Now, how about we try another exchange, and this time we both mean it?"

Lara chose that moment to step from the car. "Please take me with you. Please take me to my babies. You'll have an extra hostage." She moved toward the men, who looked confused and nervous at her unexpected play.

They didn't know what her game was. They probably weren't used to people begging them to be kidnapped.

"Lara." He tried to put as much warning into his voice as possible.

But her face, white as the moonlight, was set in a mask of determination as she marched forward, her body rigid with fear.

"Stop right there," one of the men said and raised his weapon.

The others followed his example. There was more than one finger twitching on a trigger. While most of the thugs looked like seasoned criminals, the two youngest seemed pretty green. They weren't going to be able to keep cool long under pressure. And the tension was palpable in the air. One wrong word, one wrong move could set off fireworks.

Lara took another step forward. "I'll take care of the babies while you negotiate so they won't be any trouble. It'll be easier for you." She took another step, her arms out in an entreating gesture. She had left her gun in the car.

Despite the cold, a bead of sweat rolled down Reid's temple. He could have strangled her. This was why you didn't bring a civilian to a hostage exchange, dammit. He watched as one of the younger guys locked his elbows, his eyes narrowing as he went for the shot.

Reid had no other option but to shoot first, yelling, "Get down!" to Lara at the same time.

She had enough sense to listen, hit the ground hard and roll back toward the car, accepting at last that she wasn't going to get her way.

The next second Reid was on the ground, too, returning fire. Thank God, the shots coming from the bridge divided the enemy.

Reid was almost back at the car when he was hit in the hip. Which wouldn't support his weight now to get up and out of harm's way.

Then Lara was there, pulling him inside, shoving him down behind the dashboard, taking the wheel, tearing the hell out of there, mud flying in their wake. A pro couldn't have done it better. He wished she would have shown some of this common sense and acumen five minutes earlier. But just when he thought she was finally getting with the program, she slowed the car.

"Are you all right?" she asked.

His hip burned enough to take his breath away. "Go,

go, go! Don't stop for anything. What the hell were you thinking?"

She slowed even more. "I can't leave my babies. I can leave you out here. You can call for an ambulance. I have to go back, Reid."

She was a wild one, whether she wanted to be or not. Had more of her grandmother's blood in her than she thought. No civilian in her right mind would want to go back into a hail of bullets once she'd been lucky enough to escape.

"They don't have the kids," he ground out the words.

"Are you sure?"

"A hundred percent. Honey, if I weren't, you couldn't have dragged me out of there if you'd tied me to the trailer hitch."

She held his gaze for a long moment, then stepped on the gas at last, a fat tear rolling down her face. She wiped it away angrily. "What do we do next? We're not giving up. I can't give up, Reid."

"Nobody's giving up. We'll reestablish the parameters. Raise the stakes." He was dialing his cell phone already. "Hi, Eileen. I'm Reid Graham. Thank you again for handing that CD over like you did. You've been a great help. Listen, we've hit a snag here and we have an emergency on our hands. Two little kids were kidnapped recently. We believe your sister's boyfriend had a hand in it. We have to get to these kids and quickly. Can you tell me everything you know about Kenny?"

The FBI had already asked her those questions when

they'd first begun investigating Kenny, but back then she hadn't answered, not wanting to incriminate her sister.

"Of course. Let me think," she said now.

Apparently, Jen's death had changed things.

"Even the smallest detail might be helpful. Start with the first time you ever heard of him, ever met him."

"I only met him a couple of times. He was very, you know, just not like the family. Very condescending toward women. Had that whole male superiority going. He got the idea pretty fast that the family wasn't crazy about him and he stopped coming around. Ordered Jen to stop seeing us, too. It was like he had a hold on her she couldn't shake." She sniffed.

"So before things went sour, what did you talk about? Did he say anything about his family?"

The FBI had tried in vain to track down Kenny's family. They'd figured maybe they could get to him through his kin, but they'd given up on that path eventually and decided to go with the girlfriend angle, bringing Reid in.

"He didn't say much about his family," Eileen recalled. "My mom asked one time, and he just said his parents were dead and his brothers were scattered. I don't even know how many brothers he has."

Two. Both hidden, probably living under assumed names.

"But one time I was talking to Jen on the phone. I used to call her anyway. Screw Kenny. And I could hear two men come into the room, and I thought it was

Kenny's voice, calling the other guy bro. Then he asked who Jen was talking to. And she said she was making a hair appointment and she hung up. That's the kind of control he had over her."

"Do you know where she was at that time?"

"At Robby's up on Route 11. She said one of Kenny's friends owned the place. They were picking up something from the back office. Does that help?"

"Maybe. Thank you. And if you remember anything else, would you please call me? I'd really appreciate it."

Eileen promised, and he thanked her again and hung up at last, then punched *Robby's* into the GPS. He'd heard of the place before. It was a seedy roadside bar. Not bad. They could be there in under an hour.

He dialed Cade. "Hey, thanks for the cover fire."

"You still alive?"

"Flesh wound. I think. What happened after we left?"

"You took down four. I took three more. The drivers and another guy got away."

"You didn't have to do this for me."

"I was just going to watch," he said with a sigh. "I miss the action. Don't tell Bailey. And call if you need anything else."

"You bet," he said, although both knew he wouldn't. They were way over the line on this one. Seven bodies. The colonel would be livid. Reid swore under his breath. The FBI would want his head on a plate. He'd gone rogue, as far as they were concerned. There were going to be consequences. He didn't have time to worry about it.

"Where are you now?" Cade was asking.

He gave his location.

"I know the place. There's a small hospital in the next town, right on the main road. I did security consulting for them as a favor to a friend. Go to the E.R. and check in as Jones Smith. I'll take care of the rest."

"I'm fine."

"I saw you. You can hardly stand. Your kids need a father."

He couldn't argue with that. "Nice hit below the belt," he mumbled.

"You're already hit below the belt. Don't be stupid. Have them take care of it."

And because Cade was right—this wasn't about only him, this was about Lara and Zak and Nate—Reid decided to do it. Of course, Lara insisted on going into the emergency room with him. He only put up a token protest since he couldn't walk without leaning on her. He hated having to lean on anybody. He especially hated having to lean on Lara Jordan, because he was supposed to be protecting her, dammit.

He bit the inside of his cheek against the pain and limped through the crowded waiting room up to the window. "Jones Smith," he said.

"Oh." An older woman looked at him above the rim of her mother-of-pearl glasses. "Dr. Mifflin was just out here looking for you. He said you can go straight back as soon as you get here. He said no paperwork was needed?" She looked confused.

"He has all my stuff on file."

"Insurance papers?"

"I'm set. This way?" He looked toward the swinging doors.

"Yes. Do you need a wheelchair?"

He shot her a look that could have withered an oak tree.

"Down, Rambo," Lara whispered next to him.

Dr. Mifflin saw them immediately, took the bullet out and shot him full of antibiotics, closed the wound, asked no questions. So far, perfect. Without Cade's intervention, Reid would have had to show papers, go on record and the doctor would have called the cops, as required by law, since he was treating a gunshot wound. That would have brought a delay Reid couldn't afford.

"Thanks, Doc." He moved off the examining table.

But the physician said, "I'd like to keep you overnight for observation."

"I'd like you to give me enough drugs to numb my hip so I can function for the next forty-eight hours."

"I would advise against it."

"Duly noted."

"That's what I thought. Cade said you were in the middle of something important. My brother is a marine. Good luck."

The doctor gave him two shots, one in the front of his left hip, one in back. By the time the doctor had packed up a handful of syringes and vials for his future doses, his hip was numb. Reid thanked him and walked out of the room without needing Lara's help. Unfortunately, by the time they'd reached the exit, his left leg was numb down to the knee. By the time they'd reached the car, he couldn't feel his left foot. Not good. Every once in a while, he had this response to certain painkillers, but never before to the one he'd just been given. Figured.

And Cade's car was a stick shift.

He glanced at Lara, at the tight look on her face, the deep worry in her violet eyes. The last couple of days had been hell for her. And he had a feeling the worst wasn't over yet. She didn't need anything else to worry about. She didn't need to know that he was half-incapacitated.

He limped to the passenger door and leaned against it casually, held out the keys. "I'm bushed. I wouldn't mind catching a half-hour nap. How would you like to drive, honey?"

WITH THE DRUGS, REID couldn't feel his left leg. Without the drugs, his hip hurt too much to put any weight on it. Luckily, by the time they'd reached Robby's, a ratty old shack in the middle of a gravel parking lot just off the highway, the drugs had begun to wear off a little, so he was in some kind of in-between zone where he was able to function.

The bar was closed, but there was an apartment upstairs. He decided to take his chances. Even if Kenny's brother wasn't here, if he was a regular at the bar, the owner—the most likely person to live above the place—should have an idea where he lived. And Reid knew a dozen tricks to get the man to share that information with him.

"You stay in the car," he told Lara.

"I don't think so. You're hurt. You need backup."

"I'm fine. And I need backup out here. I'll go in through the door. If the bastard comes out a window or something, I want you to stop him."

The look she gave him was full of suspicion. Rightly so. Considering that the apartment's windows were a good twenty-five feet off the ground, he didn't think whoever was up there was going to jump. "We can't afford to lose this guy," he said before Lara could realize the same thing. And then he hauled off, not giving her any more time to think. Not giving whoever was up there time to spot their car and run.

The staircase wound up the outside of the building. He moved quietly and didn't bother knocking. Instead, he smashed his shoulder into the door and busted it. Then he was inside.

Someone was sleeping on a couch. A form shifted under the blankets.

"FBI. Hands in the air!" Reid flipped on the lights, registered the weapon on the coffee table at the same time the guy moved toward it.

"Hands in the air!"

The man swore and stood, hatred burning in his dark eyes. Most of his face was hidden behind a scraggly beard.

Reid moved forward and took the weapon, stuck it in the back of his waistband.

"Get on your stomach on the floor." He had to shove the man to make him comply. Cuffing him—hands and feet both—took only a second, but it was a second too long. He could hear a window open in another bedroom.

Reid rushed into a bedroom, gun drawn. Too late. All he could see was the blur of a guy's back as he vaulted through the window.

Dammit!

Reid leaned out the window, but couldn't shoot at him. The bastard was smart enough to pull under the awning on the back of the building that had made his escape possible. He was on the side opposite where Reid had left Lara with the car.

Except the first thing Reid had seen outside was that, although the car was still there, Lara was missing.

He took the stairs three at a time, trying to ignore the pain. Maybe Lara had heard the window open and gone around. She was a good shot, but anyone could be taken by surprise. And the guy was probably armed to the teeth.

He was pretty cool during missions. Someone had once compared him to the iceberg that sank the *Titanic*. But now his heart was going a mile a minute and he was sweating. He flew around the corner as fast as his leg allowed. Couldn't see a damn thing from behind a stack of wood piled against the wall, and beer crates that stood like small hills.

Then he cleared those and saw Lara at last. She stood with her back to him, legs apart in the stance he'd taught her, gun pointed at a prone figure on the ground. Man, she was the hottest thing he'd seen in a long time. Probably ever.

"Don't move an inch." Her voice was a little shaky, but loud enough to show she meant business.

Heat shot to Reid's loins. It seemed to be a chronic condition for him around her.

"I think I broke my leg," the man moaned, clearly in pain.

Reid moved closer. "It's the least of your problems, believe me." He grinned. Damn if it wasn't his lucky day. The resemblance was unmistakable. The man on the ground looked like he could have been Kenny's twin. He wasn't, in fact. He had to be his younger brother, Billy. The other one, Joey, was bald as a bowling ball and just as thick. Kenny was the brains of the family. Scary thought. Billy was the baby they all protected. Perfect.

He bent over the punk and looked at the leg. "Tough break, man. Something like this, you don't get it set quick, you might not walk again."

The man swore.

"You won't walk for sure if the other breaks, too. Or you can tell me where Kenny is and we can head to the nearest hospital."

This time the answer was shorter. Two words only. The first one started with *F*.

Reid shifted his weight to his left, which about killed

him. The painkillers were wearing off with lightning speed. He lifted his right leg over the man, ready to stomp. "I'm kind of in a hurry."

"Wait. I don't know where he is. I swear. I don't know. I haven't seen him in two days. When he wants to talk to me he just stops in."

Reid nudged Billy's injured leg with his toe. The guy screamed. He wasn't as tough as his older brothers, for sure. Reid shook his head. "The baby of the family."

In some sense. Certainly not in others. He was a member of the same antigovernment cell Kenny was in, wanted for the brutal beating of a state government employee up in Harrisburg and for the rape of another.

He reached into the idiot's back pocket with distaste, pulled out a cell phone, handed it to him. "I'm sure you have a way to reach your brother in an emergency."

"I don't. I swear."

He had little patience for this clown. His little boys were somewhere out there in the hands of people just like this criminal, and it scared the living daylights out of Reid. "You can call now, or I can kick your swearing mouth in. Trust me, it'll be a lot harder to talk with a broken jaw and no teeth."

Billy's fingers shook as he dialed. "They got me. I'm hurt, Kenny!" he screamed into the phone like a girl.

All Reid could do was shake his head with distaste as he took the phone away from him.

"Those murderous dimwits you call your friends have something I want. I have your brother. I'm not gonna lie to you, Kenny. The boy's in bad shape. I don't think he's gonna last long. We better make this exchange quick if you want to take him to a hospital." Hell, Kenny couldn't know how bad his little brother really was. All he could hear would be Billy's moans in the background.

"What do you want, man? I have nothin'."

"You guys have two babies."

"I had nothin' to do with that. I swear!"

"I believe you. I know you love this country. You just don't agree with how it's run. Hell, half the time I don't agree with it either. But you ain't no baby killer, Kenny. Your mama raised you boys better than that." The Briggs brothers' mother had died two years back from M.S. The boys had taken it hard. It was in their FBI files. And Reid wasn't above using that information to his advantage. "She'd want you to help those babies. You know she'd want you to help your brother. And now that Jen and the baby are gone… Jen's baby would have been your mom's first grandkid…." He let his voice trail off. "Did you know Jen was pregnant?"

"She wasn't, man. She would have told me."

"She was. And believe me, your buddies didn't ask questions before they shot her. They didn't even try to miss her."

"They didn't hit her. You have it wrong. Some bastard cop hit her in a cross fire."

"Two masked men in the back of an SUV. Nobody else got a single shot off. I was there, believe me. You already lost her and the kid to all this craziness, there's no reason to lose Billy, too. Nobody expects you to sacrifice this much."

Silence stretched on the other end, then, "What do you want?"

"You lead me to those babies. That's all I need."

"I don't know where they are. I swear I don't."

"Find out. And, Kenny? Don't do anything stupid. Think of it this way. Whatever your buddies have planned can always be done another day. Whatever they want to blow up or damage will still be there next week, and the week after that. Your little brother might not be."

"I'll get you what you need." The voice on the other end was decidedly subdued. "Don't hurt Billy."

"Hell, no. I wouldn't do that. I didn't want him hurt in the first place. He jumped out the window when he heard me coming. I'll make sure he's made comfortable until you call me back. Then if I get what I want, you get him."

Reid hung up halfway through Kenny's promises that he wasn't going to double-cross him. He put Billy's phone in his pocket next to Kenny's and his own. Then he bent down again, gripped the hoodlum's bad leg by the ankle and yanked straight down as hard as he could.

Billy howled loud enough to be heard a mile away. Then stopped. "What the hell did you do?" His small eyes were moist.

"On second look, your leg wasn't broke. It was only dislocated." He handcuffed this crook, too, then yanked him to his feet. "Who's your buddy upstairs?"

Another round of swearing spewed forth.

"Hey." Reid shoved him toward the car. "Just because your leg isn't broken, it doesn't mean it can't be." But he didn't push the issue. If Billy was even slightly less stupid than he looked, he could easily give a false name.

Instead, he shoved the guy into the backseat, then called 9-1-1. The local cops could handle his comrade upstairs.

"What is the nature of your emergency?"

"There's a known member of a domestic terrorist group in the upstairs apartment at Robby's on Route 11." Then he hung up. He was only guessing, but the guy had been sleeping on the couch at Billy's place and carrying a weapon. Reid's instincts said he was hiding from the law. And Reid trusted his instincts.

He got in behind the wheel.

Lara took the passenger seat. "I could drive."

"I'm fine." His leg was pulsing with pain, but at least it was functional. At some point he'd have to give himself another shot, but not yet. "Actually, you did good back there. You did great."

Her face lit up. "Really? I was nervous."

"It didn't show."

"Like hell," came from the back. "If my leg didn't go out, I would have toasted the bitch."

Reid glanced in the rearview mirror and locked his gaze on Billy. "You better shut your mouth if you want to keep those teeth."

Reid pulled back onto the highway and drove north, toward a string of small towns. He figured they could all use some breakfast, and especially coffee. Before long he could hear sirens in the distance, then see the flashing lights. A half dozen cop cars flew by him.

Billy swore. Reid looked at him in the rearview mirror. The guy shut up. Apparently, he did like his teeth.

LARA WAS STILL SHAKING inside. She'd never held a weapon on a person before. She hadn't been sure if her knees would hold up. Billy was right. If he hadn't hurt his leg, he would probably have taken her out with no trouble.

But she'd contained the situation somehow, by the grace of God, and then Reid had been there, his speech transforming to redneck talk when he spoke to Kenny. Probably to establish a rapport. An FBI trick? Even his posture had changed. It was like she hadn't even known him.

She didn't know him, she reminded herself for the hundredth time. He always worked undercover. He could probably switch between personalities with ease. He could be playing a role even now, with her, and she would never know it. Except something told her that the way he'd been with her for the last couple of days *was* the real Reid. And she was fast becoming as attracted to this new Reid as she'd been to the old one. Or more so, God help her.

"Hey. Zak and Nate are fine," he was telling her. "We'll have them back soon. Whatever it takes." He reached for her hand, his long fingers wrapping around hers. "I promise."

And even though he hadn't always been straight with her in the past, she trusted that promise. Because whatever role he'd played before, whatever role he might be playing now, she was beginning to recognize some core deep inside the man, a core that never changed. He was tough, he never hesitated to put his life on the line for others, he made her feel…

If Billy hadn't been in the back, she would have scooted across the seat to lean against Reid. The last remnants of her anger toward him having evaporated when she wasn't looking, every part of her craved the strength and comfort he offered.

He was going to break her heart all over again, she realized. Only this time it would be worse, because what she felt for him was no longer a mixture of girlish lust and a crush. She was a woman, falling in love with the man who was the father of her children.

Chapter Ten

By the time they stopped at a drive-through and got some food and coffee, Kenny was calling. "I think I know where you need to go."

Reid gripped the phone. "I'm listening."

"I want Billy first."

"Now, you know that's not going to happen. We'll do an even exchange, how about that? You tell me where those babies are. I'll go see if you're right. If what you say checks out, you get Billy."

"I wanna be with him while you go, then. I wanna see my brother."

Easier than he'd hoped for. Reid suppressed a smile. "That's fair. So where do we set this up? Should be close to where the babies are."

Silence filled the line while Kenny thought things over. "North of Philly."

"Anywhere particular?"

"That's all you get until I see Billy."

"I trust you. You know the racetrack up there?"

"Sure."

"Let's meet in the back of the parking lot. By the

hot dog stands. And, Kenny? Let's not mess this up. There's too much at stake for the both of us."

HE WAS THERE BY 9:00 a.m. The whole place was empty. Lara was dozing on and off in the passenger seat. They hadn't gotten nearly enough sleep. Snow began to fall. Reid's hip was pulsing with pain. He pushed the car door open, needing to get out and test if he could stand. He stopped when his phone rang.

"How's it going?" Cade asked.

"I'm about to trade one of their guys for information on where the twins are."

"Need help?"

"You have a pregnant wife at home who'll skin you if you get back in the business."

"Truth is," Cade said with a chuckle, "it's my pregnant and beautiful wife who's making me call. I had to come clean. We made a promise to each other about honesty. If I do something she hates enough that she bashes my head in with an iron skillet, those are the risks I have to take. But I'm not going to lie to her. Never had, won't start now."

"Good strategy. But, seriously. You don't have to do this. It's not your fight."

"So anyway, I told her about the twins. And you know how pregnant women are. *Ouch.* So anyway, I'm coming to help."

Reid still hesitated a moment before he said, "We're at the old Giorgio Brothers' Racetrack. I'll brief you when you get here." Truth was, having Cade with him would give him options he wouldn't have otherwise. It would make all the difference.

His phone rang again almost as soon as he'd hung up. "What the hell are you doing?" his FBI handler shouted. "I want you to come in. I want you to come in and bring the Jordan woman with you. If you're not in by noon, I'm considering this a kidnapping. You hear me, Graham? This is not one of your wild commando ops where anything goes. Your damn colonel says he ordered you to return. Where the hell have you been? Did you have anything to do with the 9-1-1 call up on Route 11 this morning?"

"What call?"

"Don't play dumb, Graham. Cops found Ron Rollins cuffed and yelling that his friend was kidnapped. Billy Briggs. Kenny Briggs's little brother. Hell of a coincidence."

"Stranger things have happened. Any news on Ben?" He was pretty messed up when the EMTs had taken him out of that safe house, but he was a tough operator. Reid's money was on him.

"He's going to make it. You just focus on Billy Briggs and Lara Jordan. That's two counts of kidnapping so far," Adams warned. "Don't think the FBI is going to go easy on you because you've been so helpful. Once you go rogue, that's all forgotten."

"There you go making me feel all warm and fuzzy inside. You know how much I hate that."

"By noon," Adams gritted out the words. "And

everyone you have in your custody better be with you. Unharmed. Am I clear?"

"Crystal."

CADE ARRIVED AROUND 10:00 a.m. Reid got out and limped across the parking lot with him, strategizing, while he trusted Lara to hold her gun on Billy.

"I'm not going to miss," she warned again when Billy fidgeted, his eyes shifting all over the place. "And even if I did, those two won't. They'll shoot you dead the second you step foot outside of this car."

He swore at her at length, including enough family members for a reunion.

She let it roll off her.

Then, eventually, Cade came back and took over. "Reid wants to talk to you," he said.

She crossed the lot to him. A precaution, she supposed, to be far from the car so Billy wouldn't hear them. Reid stood just a little differently than usual, favoring his bad hip. The tight lines around his mouth told her how much standing there cost him.

But when he spoke, there was no trace of pain in his voice, never a sign of weakness. "The best thing would be if you stayed here with Cade. You could help him keep an eye on Billy. Kenny, too, when he gets here."

"I'm going to be wherever Zak and Nate are. If you're trying to sell me on the idea that Cade will be outnumbered, and he needs me to help him, I'm going to be really offended. How stupid do you think I am?"

"Too smart for your own good." He pressed his lips

together. "Okay, how about if I ask you to stay for the sake of your own safety?"

"Not a chance."

"How did I know that you were going to say that?"

"Because I'm a strong, independent woman?"

"That you are. Exactly like your grandmother."

"Really?" She felt a smile tug at the corners of her mouth.

"But even so, please don't do anything reckless." He reached out and pulled her to him, brushed his lips across hers, rested his forehead against hers. "I couldn't stand it if something happened to you."

Warmth spread through her at his sudden confession. Because the truth was, in the last couple of days, she'd started to feel—

"You're the mother of my children."

She swallowed her disappointment. *The mother of his children.* She was that. But she was afraid that things had gone beyond that. She was also the woman falling in love with him. Well, who needed that complication? Nobody. Especially not now. She pressed her lips together and forced a small smile. She was going to keep her idiot heart under control if it killed her.

The snow picked up. She blinked a fat flake off her eyelashes.

Reid pulled away, but kept one hand on her arm. "Okay, when Kenny gets here, I'll have him get in the back with his brother. Cade will stay and hold them until we know for sure whether the twins are here or not."

"Sounds like a plan."

"Be careful. No insane heroics like at the bridge."

She flashed him a look. "I knew you'd bring that up. I had to try something. I thought they had the twins and they were just going to drive away. Might not have been the smartest thing to do. Thanks for not jumping down my throat about it."

He gave a sour smile. "You don't know what it cost me not to bring it up until now. I could have—" He shook his head. "You didn't get hurt. That's what matters."

A small smile spread across her lips as she processed his words. "What, no macho yelling and I'm-the-boss speech? I think you're growing."

"Don't tell anyone."

He watched her, an unreadable expression on his face. Then he pulled her back to him and kissed her like he meant it. And she responded fully, her twisted emotions and her desperation giving the kiss an edge.

They only pulled apart when Cade beeped the horn behind them. A red pickup was coming down the road toward the gates.

Kenny was here.

THE PLACE KENNY SENT THEM was two exits up the highway, down Slaughterhouse Road. Reid parked Cade's white SUV—the perfect color for the rapidly whitening landscape—way up the road, and pulled in among the bushes. He and Lara walked up to an abandoned slaughterhouse on foot—his hip hurting like hell—through the shrubs that had overtaken the holding pens nobody had used in a decade.

Most of the fences were down, covered by dead weeds and snow. The building was in the same deplorable condition. The steel roof was rusty and peeled back in places. Some of the windows were boarded up, some plain missing.

The front doors, which were ten feet tall and wide enough to drive a truck through, were held together by a thick chain and padlock. There were a number of other, smaller entrances on the side. They headed toward the one where the bushes were tallest, providing them with the best cover.

"Should we separate and circle the place?" Lara whispered. Like him, she had her gun out, at the ready.

He shook his head, shifting the bag of weapons on his shoulder. He wanted to keep her in his sight for as long as possible. "We don't separate."

They reached the building, and he noted footprints in the snow that made a path around the structure. Looked like whoever was in there was cautious enough to check the perimeter from time to time. Reid held her back with one hand, turned the doorknob with the other.

"Locked."

But someone was definitely in there. As he heard voices, he lifted his hand to signal Lara to be quiet. A few men were talking. Arguing. Three or four, he would have guessed, but couldn't be sure. And he needed to be. Walking into a situation like this, surprises weren't a good thing.

If he were alone, trying to retrieve some weapon or sensitive documents, he would have busted in. But Lara was here with him. And there was a chance that his little boys were inside. Which meant that a lot more recon work and planning was needed.

He pulled back into the brush and began walking to the left, rounding the building, Lara close behind him. Every time he came to a door, he tried it as quietly and carefully as he could. Every time, he got the same result.

They were locked up tight in there.

He looked up. No obvious way to climb, not without equipment and without making too much noise. The metal siding was no help.

He considered every option carefully. Big place. Way too big to hold just two little babies. They could have other things here. Their headquarters, their arsenal, a freaking tank, whatever.

There was the main door, two side doors and two emergency exits. Now that they'd fully circled the place, he had an exact count. The windows were all too high to see through. Not much help, but useful in another way. Nobody could look out and see him coming either.

When he heard the sounds of a car pulling up, they inched up to the front again and watched from around the corner, hidden behind the bushes. After a brief knock, three more men walked into the slaughterhouse through one of the side doors. They'd left the car running.

"Jimmy Sparks," Lara whispered behind him.

Oh, he'd recognized the bastard—same shaved head and red goatee he'd worn back in Hopeville. Reid's muscles drew tight. He could feel the burn on his skin all over again. The thought that the thug would come anywhere near his children made him want to tear Sparks apart with his bare hands, from limb to limb.

He considered his options. He could call in the FBI. They would grab him first and take him out of the operation and off the scene. Adams was mad as hell at him. They would come with force. There'd be negotiations, which Sparks could resist. He'd proven over and over that he would do anything not to get caught. A shoot-out was a distinct possibility.

Reid shifted to ease the pain that seemed now to be pulsating through his whole body. He thought about calling the colonel instead of the FBI. Except that would get the SDDU in trouble. Not to mention that few SDDU soldiers were stateside at any given time. Mostly they were deployed, deep undercover overseas. They were only brought back to the States for debriefings in between missions or, if they were injured, to recuperate.

He looked at the building again. There could be a number of surprises waiting in there. Risks he would have taken as a lone-wolf commando soldier—hell, he would have enjoyed the challenge. But with Lara and the boys…

He didn't like it.

There were too many people inside, and he'd have to go in blind, prepared for every possibility. Such as the chance that this was a trap, and Zak and Nate weren't in there, after all. Kenny could have set him up.

This sure didn't look like what he'd pictured as the endgame. He'd figured the twins had been passed off to the wife of somebody in the group. Some woman who already had other children and had the necessary stuff in her house. He'd planned on making sure she was alone, then going in. She wouldn't do anything foolish. She would hand the twins over without trouble, to protect her own kids.

But this place…

The more he looked at it, the surer he was that Kenny had to be either up to no good or mistaken.

The sound of a baby crying came from inside the building.

Reid swore under his breath, a wave of emotion slammed through his chest, as Lara whispered, "That's Zak."

He was on the phone already, giving Cade the go-ahead to take the Briggs brothers in.

Instinct pushed him to bust through the nearest door. Experience held him back. Since Sparks and his men had left the car running, it probably meant they didn't plan to be there long. The smartest move would be to wait until they left, even the odds a little.

For a second, he wondered again if he should have called in the troops so Sparks could be picked up. But he was within feet of the twins. No way he would let anyone sweep in now and take over the op, pull him off. If they made some blundering mistake…

He punched Sparks's license plate number into his cell phone and sent it off to his handler as a compromise. It was the best he could do under the circumstances.

Half an hour passed before Sparks and his entourage

exited the building, with one extra guy joining them. The man walked the others to the car, but didn't get in. They talked another minute before Sparks and his men left. Then the guy walked back to the side door they'd used and pulled out his cell.

The door was open.

Reid signaled Lara to stay back, leaving his bag of weapons with her as he inched closer. But he couldn't get close enough to take a look inside. If he went too close to the edge of the boxwood bushes that were his cover, the goon on the phone would see him. And he couldn't grab the guy either. The others inside would see through the open door.

"No, your mother can't take the kids to get their picture taken with Santa," the guy was saying. "Because I said so, dammit. She can have her own damn picture if she wants." He began to pace. "End of conversation." He pulled a pack of cigarettes out of his pocket. "Yeah, I know it's still snowing. No, I ain't coming home. Grab the shovel and get out in the driveway."

One more foot. Reid watched, ready to lunge.

Then froze in place.

Kenny's phone was buzzing in Reid's pocket. He'd set both phones to vibrate.

He held his breath, but the guy pacing in front of him was too busy with his own conversation to hear anything else.

Reid stayed still. His hip burned with such pain he could barely stand, but he compartmentalized it. He didn't care what damage he was doing to himself, as long as he could complete this one mission successfully. Nothing mattered beyond his boys.

Then the guy did take that extra step, turned his back to pace the other way. Reid hooked one hand over his mouth, the other over his neck and hauled him into the bushes. He broke his neck before Lara came up to them, was answering the call on Kenny's phone the next second.

"Be at the Easton train station in an hour. Have everything with you and ready." The line went dead.

He had no intention of following those directions when he was this close to his children.

Lara was looking at the dead guy at his feet, her face the color of the white-gray sky above. The gun trembled in her hand. "What did they say?"

"Playing more of their games. Doesn't matter." *She shouldn't be here.*

But, as if she could hear his thoughts, she pulled her shoulders straight. Her hands steadied. "I can handle this."

"I couldn't just tie him up and risk him making noise, or knocking him out and risk him coming out of it and somehow attacking us from behind."

"You don't have to explain. We're here to do whatever it takes." Her gaze hardened.

She had stood up to the test at every turn. Admiration for her indomitable spirit rose in him, even as he regretted that she had to be tested. He'd never given much thought to having children, hadn't thought that would ever be an issue. But now that he had Zak and Nate, he couldn't imagine a better mother to raise them. He was a lucky man in that regard, for sure.

Somehow he'd ended up with a fine family. And for a moment, he wished he could keep them. Then he shook off that selfish thought.

He grabbed the guy's black baseball cap and shoved it onto his own head. Their jackets already matched for the most part—camouflage. Reid moved back toward the door. Lara followed closely behind, for as long as he let her, leaving her in the cover of the bushes.

He moved forward alone, bracing himself for anything, stepping into view, moving into the open doorway. He held one hand to his ear as if talking on a phone, keeping the other near his gun, presenting his back to the door, only turning his head a fraction to catch glimpses in his peripheral vision.

Hoses snaked on the floor around rows of drains. Giant meat hooks hung from the ceiling. Stainless steel processing stations stood in rows a little further in, stainless steel tubs in between them. Here and there in stacks of various sizes, what looked like emergency food rations were piled up in apple crates. Bags of flour, potatoes, bottled water and other supplies. Looked like the place was the cell's pantry for a prolonged emergency.

Reid kept his head down and turned. Spotted a rickety crib by a space heater. A middle-aged woman sat next to it, smoking and reading a tabloid magazine. She wore a quilted jacket, her greasy hair pulled back in a ponytail, bangs teased up within an inch of their lives. He ran the pictures of all known female members of the cell through his mind, but didn't come up with a match. Of course, the FBI's list of the cell's members was more than sketchy.

He made some noises as if agreeing to something over the phone. He couldn't say anything or the four guys strategizing over a card table would know that the voice was wrong. They were in a shadowy corner, so he had to strain to see their faces. One looked familiar from the FBI files. None of them had been there at the bridge, as far as he could tell.

"Shut the damn door," another, lying on a cot in the corner, yelled over.

He stepped back out, pretending to still be on the phone, and shut the door behind him.

"Zak and Nate?" Lara held her breath, her gaze begging when he returned to her.

"They looked unharmed."

Her shoulders relaxed a fraction. "How many men?"

"Five guys. Plus a babysitter."

"Now we call for backup?"

He shook his head. "No time for that. Sparks and his goons could come back at any time."

"Cade?"

"Can't afford to wait for him."

"But the odds…" Worry was fixed in her eyes.

He knew she didn't fear for herself. She was anguished about the babies. "These odds we can live with." He squatted and drew the outline of the building in the snow. "I'll shoot my way through the door and go in here." He pointed at the door that was closest to the men where he'd last seen them. "That will surprise them. They'll be confused for a second. When you hear the shots, count to five, then come through this door." He pointed to the unlocked door behind him.

She nodded. "By the time they recover from the surprise, I'll divide their attention."

"Right."

She could do this, he told himself as he pulled a syringe from his pocket, ripped the sterile packaging off, drew the drug from the vial the doctor had given him. He pulled down the waist of his pants a few inches, then shoved the needle in. The area began to go numb almost immediately. Better get moving so he would have full use of his window of opportunity.

He capped the needle and shoved it back in his pocket then grabbed his bag of weapons, although he knew most of them would be useless. He couldn't lob hand grenades with those babies in there. "I'll get the men. You take care of the babysitter."

She was vibrating with nerves. "Any last-minute advice?"

"Keep count of your bullets."

SHE KEPT ONE EYE on the door, the other on the road, hoping Jimmy wouldn't come back. Then shots sounded from the other end of the building. She walked from her cover to the door. "One. Two. Three. Four. Five." Opened door. Screamed, "Police!"

She had no idea why she'd said that. They hadn't

talked about it. Her nerves were shot, her mind following some blueprint of attack she'd only seen on TV. One man was on the ground, another shooting at Reid with one hand, clutching his knee with the other. Her mind registered all this in a split second, along with the crib. Then she remembered the plan and dove for cover, avoiding, at the last second, the bullets that flew her way.

They pelted the stainless steel workstation, cut through, but none of them hit her—a miracle. When a few seconds passed without more of them coming, she peeked out. Another man was on the ground. Everyone had taken cover. Only the crib stood out there in the open.

Someone had knocked over an old box behind the crib, rusty tools lay scattered on the floor. She would have to watch out for those when she ran. She couldn't afford to trip.

She could see Reid making a move behind cover to get to the back of the remaining men. She drew a deep breath and ran for the next workstation, then the next, each bringing her closer to her crying babies. Each time she was in the open, she shot indiscriminately, making sure she wouldn't hit Reid or the crib, but to cause enough ruckus that the enemy stayed down and wouldn't give her any trouble.

Her heart beat out of control. Sweat rolled down her face. Her knees were knocking. She ignored all that and kept her focus locked on the twins. They were standing in the crib, nothing but their fuzzy heads showing, bawling their eyes out. *They're not hurt, just scared. They're not hurt, just scared.*

A shout came from behind her. "Watch out." Reid took aim at the man who was targeting her. But to do that, he had to pop up from cover. He shot the guy threatening her at the same time that the last remaining man shot Reid in the shoulder. The impact of the bullet knocked him over.

A woman came forward from somewhere with a cry and held her gun on Lara, moving toward her with grim determination.

No way. Not when she was this close. Lara lifted her own weapon and squeezed the trigger.

Nothing happened.

In the chaos and sheer insanity of the attack, she'd forgotten to count her bullets. She stood there, stunned and not knowing what to do next. By the mercy of God, the other woman seemed to be in no better shape.

Her hands were shaking, tears streaking down her face. One of the injured men must have meant something to her. She kept coming closer on unsteady legs, probably wanting to make sure she wouldn't miss her target.

Behind Lara, Reid was busy with his own duel. She threw her gun as hard as she could at the woman, knocking the attacker's weapon aside for a second. It was enough for Lara to lunge and take her down hard. A shot did get squeezed off as they rolled, both grunting, but it only hit the ceiling.

Zak and Nate were screaming, scared to death. The

woman fought to bring her gun down and take aim. Lara rolled her again, one of the rusty tools digging painfully into her back. Then the woman rolled, too, slamming Lara's head against the wall. She was stunned just enough for her grip to weaken. The woman pulled away, lifted the gun. But Lara's fingers closed around a cleaver on the floor. The next second it was buried in the woman's chest, a surprised look on her face as she folded without ever firing her weapon.

Reid took out his guy, too, at last, blood running down his arm. But she only had eyes for her babies. Lara was at the crib in two steps, grabbing up the twins, looking them over. "Mommy is here. Mommy is here." She kissed every available inch of those two precious little boys. "Shh. We're okay now. Everything's okay. I missed you so much."

Then Reid was beside her, bleeding worse from the left shoulder than she'd thought at first glance, looking like his left leg wasn't completely supporting him.

He was checking them over, touching her, running his hands over the babies. "Are you okay? The kids?"

"How badly are you hurt?"

"I'm ready to put my feet up." His lips were tight with pain. But when guns went off outside suddenly, he stepped in front of them and was ready to start fighting all over again.

The budding love Lara felt for him, the one she'd been trying to stifle, welled in her chest.

"Probably Sparks and his goons." Reid stood strong and tall, ready to lay down his life for them. "Take the boys, go out the back door. And don't stop running."

Chapter Eleven

The door opened and more men entered. From the corner of his eyes, Reid saw that Lara was trapped. She squatted with the babies, using her own body as their cover. His muscles stiffened as he readied to fight for everything he held dear. But the shadow appearing in the door, coming in low with gun drawn, seemed familiar.

"If you tell me I'm late, I'm going to be ticked," Cade called from the other end of the cavernous building as he straightened, taking in the bodies that littered the ground.

Reid backed up to a workstation and leaned against it, taking the weight off his bad hip. "What was that outside?"

Lara sat on the floor, her legs giving out at last. The babies quieted and snuggled tight to her chest, everything right in their little world as long as their mother was here.

He moved toward her as Cade said, "I pulled in and was about to come through the door when a black pickup came down the road and started shooting at me."

"Did you get them?" Reid only had eyes for Lara and the boys.

"Bastards took off the second they realized I meant business." Sirens about drowned out his last words.

"The FBI followed you after you dropped off Kenny and Billy?" Dismay shot through Reid. This was why he always worked alone. "Damn, man. This happens when you retire. You lose it," he was only half joking.

Cade was examining his feet.

Suspicion had Reid doing a double take. "You let them follow you?"

Cade shuffled. "I figured, this was it, the endgame. I thought they might come in handy. Look man, I know how you get about asking for help, but it's not a crime, all right? When you need it, you need it."

For a second, Reid bristled. He didn't *need* anyone or anything. On principle. But he didn't have it in him to be angry for long. At this stage, whoever was coming couldn't do too much damage. He glanced toward the back door. "I want to take Zak and Nate to get checked out."

"Then you'd better go now. If you stay, they won't let you leave for a while. I'll stay and explain things."

"You know you'll catch hell for this, right?"

"Retirement was starting to get boring anyway." Cade came closer and grinned at Lara. "Cute kids."

She grinned back. "We got them back. We kicked terrorist butt, didn't we?"

"You more than I," Cade said sourly. And when Reid chuckled, the relief hitting him all at once, Cade punched him in the shoulder. The one that wasn't bleeding. "Better get going."

"Wait. What happened to the virus?" Lara was asking.

"The vials are in a safe place," Cade told her. "The outfit we work for is set up to handle these kinds of things."

Reid took one of the boys from Lara and they ran for the back. Reid figured they had just enough time to go around and get to the car he'd left in the bushes before his leg went completely numb. Lara would have to do the driving again. For the moment, he was too happy to resent that she had to help him out. She was right, whatever else happened next, the most important thing was that Zak and Nate were safe.

As he looked at the twins, looked at her, there was only one thought on his mind: *his.* A thought he couldn't afford under any circumstances.

HE DIDN'T WANT TO SEEM presumptuous, but he wasn't ready to leave her on her own either, so once they reached a hotel Reid compromised by getting one room but with two double beds.

"I should go back to the hospital," Lara said as she came out of the bathroom. Their hotel was just down the road from where medical personnel were even now watching over their babies.

"Zak and Nate are fine. The doctor said they were only keeping them overnight for observation. You have to rest. You're half-asleep on your feet." Going home was out of the question. He could barely talk her into coming this far, less than five minutes away if they were needed.

She sank onto the bed, running a towel over her short hair. Another was wrapped around her body. "The dehydration—"

"Was fairly minor. And they both got IVs." Man, he hated to see those kids hooked up to anything, even if they took it like the brave little troupers they were.

But she'd had trouble handing over the twins, even to the doctors. Then wouldn't leave them until they were both asleep. She ran the towel over her hair one more time. "I hate that they have to go through this."

"They're fine." Reid came over from the window—he'd been watching the hotel's entrance, force of habit, although he didn't expect trouble—and sat next to her. "I think Nate is starting to like me. We played ball." He grinned.

He could tell them apart now. They might have looked a lot alike, but they had completely different personalities. Nate was take-charge, Zak was more easygoing. Reid had stopped by the gift store on his way up from the E.R.—he had gone there to have his arm treated—and pretty much bought it out as far as toys were concerned. He wanted to give them the world.

He'd felt fiercely protective of them from the moment he'd found out that they were his, but the love that had crept up on him with each second they'd spent together was on a whole other level.

"Here." He pulled a pair of sweatpants and a

sweatshirt from a bag at his feet, also from the gift shop. He'd already showered so he was wearing a matching set.

But Lara simply lay back on the bed, looking exhausted. "How are you?"

"Good as new." The doctor had patched up his shoulder and given him some pain shots for both the shoulder and his hip that didn't make him go numb, a definite advantage. He got up so he could pull the cover over her and let her get some rest.

"Stay. Please."

He did, sitting on the edge of the bed.

"Tell me about your wife."

Okay. That came out of left field. He cleared his throat as memories he'd long kept locked up flooded over him.

Lara didn't know what she was asking. Leila had been the low point of his life. Those memories still gave him nightmares. He hadn't forgiven himself for all that had happened. And had a feeling that if Lara knew the whole story, she wouldn't forgive him either.

And yet, he was the father of Lara's children. She had a right to know what kind of a man he was, even if it meant that she would hate him for the things he'd done in the past. He cleared his throat again.

"Some time ago, there was a warlord on the Afghan-Pakistani border the army was having a lot of trouble with. We got the job. A few guys got sent into different areas. I was sent to a small village in the mountains. We had an old man there who was sick of the Taliban and the warlord who was their henchman. The old man was willing to work with us. I went in undercover as his American-born grandson, coming home from the U.S. to find my heritage and faith and all that."

He drew a slow breath, remembering the day and the people clearly. "The village took me in readily enough. The warlord blew through every couple of months, taking food and recruiting. I was trying to get on his team, but he didn't trust me." He paused. "I had to get to his headquarters. We knew he was running training camps. I figured that if he wouldn't take me as one of his men, he might take me as an enemy prisoner. I started to talk against him in the village."

"Did they listen?"

He closed his eyes. "Not at first. These were people born and bred in fear. But after a while, yes. They started to look up to me and stand up for themselves. It was pretty slow progress. In the meantime, one day a man brought a young girl to me and offered her for a price. A bride price. It's common." He swallowed, still seeing the pale round face, how scared she'd been.

"And I knew if I said no, I'd offend the man, possibly the whole village, and all the progress we'd made would have been for nothing. If I said no, he would just take the girl to another man, maybe one of the warlord's men when they came by next. The family needed the money. They couldn't feed a girl who was already grown and should have been a husband's concern."

"How old was she?" Lara asked after a moment.

"Didn't know. The poorest people, up in those

mountains, they can't read or write. They don't keep close track. She was born in the winter after the earthquakes—that was all her mother told her, but they have earthquakes there pretty often. I figured her for eighteen. I was twenty-eight."

"You married her."

"To save her from a worse fate. But I didn't touch her, I swear, for a long time. Then a year passed, two. I had information on one of the training camps at last, but I was kept in place, told to keep a low profile. New intelligence came in that the warlord had more important connections than we'd thought. Connections I was supposed to discover."

"And things changed with her?"

"One day her father packed up all his belongings, every goat, rag, dish they had, to pay back the bride price—money he'd already spent—since she didn't give me any children. His honor was at stake. I could barely talk him out of turning his family into beggars. And they would have been that. He would have taken Leila to the nearest small town and sold her to be a prostitute, along with her younger sisters. He wouldn't have had any other choice.

"I negotiated more time. He thought me a fool, even accused me of wanting to humiliate him. And that night, Leila came to me, crying, begging to be allowed into my bed." He couldn't, to this day, figure out whether he let her for her sake, or his mission's, or because he'd been so incredibly lonely. And the fact that he didn't know made him feel like dirt. Which was why he kept those memories locked away.

"It's okay," Lara whispered.

"It wasn't love." That simply wasn't a requirement for marriage over there. "But I came to care for her. We'd been sharing the same house. She'd been cooking my meals, repairing my clothes. She was a smart girl. We spent a lot of evenings talking. I was a lonely man, she was a lonely young woman. She was begging me to give her a child, for herself, for her family. I wasn't sure if I could, but I thought I owed it to her to try."

"What happened to her?"

"Things went on like that for a while. Then the warlord noticed that the villagers weren't as scared of him as before, figured out that it was my influence. His men came to the house while I was away. They killed her as a warning to me. He figured I'd be suitably cowed."

"Reid..."

"When I got home—" He shook his head. "I went after him. The powers that be ordered me back. Called me into the city for debriefing. While I was gone, the warlord heard that I was out for revenge. He realized he'd misjudged me. He was afraid the village would stand behind me, and maybe other villages, too, if the news spread that his influence had weakened. So he struck first, and killed every man, woman and child." His throat closed up.

The warlord and his men were rounded up, he'd seen to that, the training camps had been shut down. But none of that made up for those graves on the hillside, an image that haunted him still. And made him question his orders every time since, making him, and probably Colonel Wilson, wonder if he was still suited for the job. He sure as hell didn't reassure the powers that be with this case.

He lay on top of the covers next to Lara. He wasn't touching her, but she had her arms around him, her head on his shoulder. He'd just confessed that over two hundred innocent people had died because of him, including his own wife, and Lara didn't tell him that he didn't deserve to be alive, a thought that had crossed his mind more than once after the tragedy.

Of course, just because she didn't think that he didn't deserve her, didn't mean that wasn't exactly the case.

He moved to get off the bed.

"Stay," she said again.

So he stayed on top of the covers beside her. Only that didn't seem enough, all of a sudden, so he took her into his arms. And, slowly, his thoughts returned from the past to the present. Here he was, dumping his dark past on her when she had to be worried sick about the twins. "Everything is going to be fine now. I promise."

Just holding her and not going any further took every ounce of his self-control. She was practically naked, her skin carrying the fresh scent of orange spice soap. But she was worn-out both in body and spirit. He wasn't going to take advantage of her under any circumstances.

Not if it killed him. Not even if she wanted him, which he was pretty sure she didn't.

He tried to think of all the flack he was going to catch for the last couple of days—a mental bucket of ice water—and held his body still.

But then she snuggled even closer. "I'm sorry about what happened to Leila and the others. I really am sorry for her, and I'm sorry that you have to carry all that around. But you saved us. You saved me and my babies. You stood in front of the bullets. And I'm grateful for that. I'm grateful that we're here, alive. I'm grateful that you didn't die on that hillside in Afghanistan and came to Hopeville."

She turned to him fully until her breasts were pressed against his chest, with precious little in the way of a barrier. He felt sweat bead on his forehead.

"I know you're tired." Her breath tickled his neck, shooting one-hundred-proof lust to key points of his body.

Worse were the powerful emotions swirling in his chest, emotions he hadn't been prepared for and didn't know what to do with.

"But if you're not, you know, completely, terribly tired…?" She pulled back, a wary look in her eyes as if she expected him to reject her.

Like that was going to happen, no matter what he'd said to himself before.

"Are you asking what I think you're asking?" he checked, to be sure. *Go slow. Whatever you do, go slow. And don't get your hopes up.*

Her only answer was a nearly imperceptible nod.

He gathered her tighter against him, until he had

trouble telling where he ended and she began. She gave a shaky smile as he leaned in to brush a kiss across her soft lips.

And then he lost it completely. So much for better judgment.

Making love with her seemed like the last thing he should be doing at the moment. But in another way, making love seemed like the only thing they could do. He pulled her even closer.

"I WANTED YOU from the moment I first laid eyes on you," he told her in between kissing her senseless.

Lara's body floated on pleasure. Zak and Nate were safe. They'd all come through the ordeal of the last couple of days alive. Reid was here, back in her life again, back in the boys' lives. A rocky road waited for them, but she didn't want to think about that now. She needed a break tonight. And Reid was doing an excellent job of making all her tension and worry melt away.

"But the whole truth is," he continued, "that I wanted you every moment since. I don't think a day passed that I didn't think of you. There were nights, in my dreams, when I could still feel your skin and taste your lips. The memory of you drove me crazy."

He tugged the towel from around her, his movements growing urgent. He immediately caught himself. "Sorry. I'm too..." He drew a slow breath, gave a shaky laugh. "Here I am, ready to devour you when what you need is slow and easy."

She kind of liked the idea that he was as starved

for her as she was for him. He wanted to slow down? Couldn't he tell that she was practically vibrating with frustration? "The last two years were pretty slow," she gave him a hint.

A glint came into his eyes as he caught it. "Are you sure?"

She slipped a hand under his sweatshirt, splaying her fingers against his washboard abdomen. "What do you think?"

The sweatshirt was gone before she could blink.

Then her bare breasts were pressed against his naked chest that was wide and gloriously muscled, dusted with the barest hint of coarse hair, which she immediately set to discover with her fingers.

He groaned deep in his throat when she came in contact with a hard, flat nipple. "You overestimate the amount of self-control I have here."

"Good thing I'm not really after self-control tonight." She hadn't had another man in her life since she'd been with him. No man after or before that night. She was more than ready.

As his hands moved all over her body, and their kissing grew more frenzied, heat and moisture pooled at the V of her thighs. Her body was ready for him. And judging from the considerable hardness jutting against her belly, he was more than ready for her.

She parted her legs.

"What about foreplay?" he murmured as he kissed his way down her neck.

"Tomorrow."

"Not to nitpick, but I think foreplay is supposed to come first."

"Good to shake things up now and then for variety." She could barely gasp out the words as his hot lips closed around her nipple.

He drew hard.

Every muscle inside her tightened.

"Our second time and you're already bringing up variety? A lesser man could develop a complex." He moved to the other nipple. "I'm just saying."

She gave a moan that was louder than she'd intended. "A lesser man couldn't make me feel like I'm about to explode any second."

"Explode, huh?" He moved down her belly. "Variety it is then. Because I'm not about to miss that train." He grabbed a foil packet from the nightstand without looking, while his mouth moved down, down, down, got in a few licks just to spite her. Her back arched, her breathing coming faster and faster. And then, he thrust into her at last with one smooth, long move, filling her, rocking into her, and she called his name as she fell into a million little pieces.

He pulled up her knees and hooked her legs over his lean hips. And pushed deeper. Then pulled out and pushed back again and again and again. The pressure inside her barely had time to abate before it began building anew. Her eyes went wide. He moved, shifted, each tiny adjustment giving a new sensation, a new kind of friction, getting her closer and closer.

Then he stopped.

"No." She pushed herself up, claiming him.

He put a hand on each side of her hips and held her immobile. "You rushed me through foreplay. Fine. But now we're slowing down a little."

"Why?"

"Because the first time, on a flour-dusted table, I didn't know you were a virgin and I went too fast. You drove me crazy. I should have taken the time to make your body melt. I should have cherished you. I should have given you everything."

"You did make my body melt. You did give me everything. I—"

He switched to slow, even thrusts that drove all argument from her mind. Fine. Slow was good. It went against instinct, the part of her that demanded release all over again. But other parts of her were really enjoying this. In fact, the pleasure seemed to build deeper the more the tension built.

Oh.

He rolled and arranged her on top. "Now you." His eyes were dark with lust. His face was focused on her, only her, making her feel like she was the most beautiful woman in the world, the *only* woman in the world.

The sensation of being on top was new, but pleasant, and then she figured out the advantages of having control, and liked it. And, of course, couldn't help picking up speed.

So he had to take control again, rolling her under him, hooking her ankles over his shoulders this time.

He was even deeper inside her now. She hadn't realized pleasure like this could exist.

"Please." The time had come. She was ready to beg shamelessly if necessary. She was a quivering mass of arousal and need, inches from disintegrating.

He pulled back and drove in a little harder. Then a little harder again and was picking up speed at last.

Then everything exploded, pleasure shooting through her like a rocket. But even that pleasure paled next to the overwhelming emotion that filled her. They were together, again, Reid and she. And this time, he didn't have any dark secrets to spirit him away from her. This time, they could stay together.

MAKING LOVE TO LARA had shaken him, opened him up in some way, left him vulnerable—a sensation he didn't care for.

"I wish you could hold me like this all night, but I'm guessing you have to leave soon to fill out paperwork and file reports or whatever." She lifted her gaze to his.

"Yes." He wouldn't lie to her. He should have left already, right after he'd seen the twins to safety at the hospital and her in the hotel. But, for the first time in his life, Reid hadn't been able to walk away. Except, eventually, he had to. "Sorry."

"Your job is what it is," she said simply, pressing a soft kiss on his injured shoulder.

The job was him. He was the job. That had always been a solid, steady point he could come back to, something he could rely on. Except, now Zak and Nate were his life, too. And Lara.

When had that happened?

This was exactly what he'd so carefully avoided since Leila. This was exactly what had killed her. And all those innocent villagers. He was a weapon in the U.S. government's arsenal. A weapon his country needed. Weapons didn't have second thoughts. Weapons didn't become emotionally involved.

He wasn't a normal guy. He wasn't husband and father material. If he got involved with her, stayed involved, she could get hurt. Zak and Nate could get hurt.

He couldn't survive that. He couldn't do his job day in, day out, knowing they might be in danger because of him. The best thing he could ever do for them would be to leave them. The sooner the better.

He'd seen what his father's disappearance had done to his mother. He knew what Leila's death had done to him. He wasn't going to do that to anyone. He'd even distanced himself from his mother over the last several years as he'd taken on increasingly dangerous assignments. The temptation for his mother, after losing her husband, was to make her son the center of her life, and she had done that for a while. But he pulled away consciously, and she had made friends and built a whole support system. He wanted her to have a normal life, whatever happened to him.

And he wanted the same thing for Lara.

Emotional connections and his job didn't mix. In his line of work, chances were he would get hurt sooner or later. He wouldn't want to cause pain to anyone. And he couldn't afford to be thinking who he might be leaving behind when he was walking into armed conflict.

He slipped out of the bed and pulled on the sweatpants, then the sweatshirt.

"Where are you going?" she asked sleepily.

"I do need to go in for that debriefing." Colonel Wilson first, then the FBI. He should have done that immediately after the shoot-out. He'd neglected his job already.

"Do you want me to wait for you so we can go over to the hospital together in the morning?"

She looked sweet and soft in the dim light, her hair tousled from their lovemaking, her tempting body outlined under the blanket. Every fiber of his being pulled him back to her. "I'm not coming back."

"Oh, okay. I'll take the boys straight home. Come by whenever you're done with your work for the day. I want to hold them for days on end and not let go. Except maybe to have their picture taken at the mall with Santa. We did that last year, too. I want to do that every year and keep the pictures so they can look back someday and see how they changed from year to year." She smiled sleepily.

She was beautiful enough for the sight of her to stop his heart.

He took a step away from the bed. "I'm not coming back," he said again, hardening his voice this time, trying to harden his heart, too, but that proved more difficult.

She sat up, wide-eyed, clutching the blanket to her chest. All the sleepiness was gone. "Ever?"

"I'll make arrangements. You'll be taken care of. I'll send word when I have everything in place." Then he turned away from her. He didn't want to see the pain on her face.

He grabbed his car keys, his wallet, his gun. Another few steps took him out of the room. He closed the door behind him, not stopping until he'd reached the elevator. He leaned his forehead against the door while he waited.

So maybe he was the stupidest, most heartless bastard in the world. But he'd done what he had to do. He was going to protect and take care of the people who were most important to him, from afar. It was better for them that way.

As far as he went, he had to trust that eventually he would learn to live with the pain.

Chapter Twelve

Nearly two days had passed since he'd last seen her. And those two days had pretty much driven him out of his mind.

He'd spent half a day debriefing the colonel, making sure he minimized Cade's participation so he wouldn't get into too much trouble. Colonel Wilson had given Reid a lot of hard and mean looks, dressed him down, cut him to size and then, instead of punishing him, had given him two weeks stateside for recuperation before he would be sent overseas on his next mission.

His FBI debriefing was worse. It'd been a long time since he'd heard that much yelling. He was kicked off the Jimmy Sparks case, naturally, which he very much regretted since he'd been itching to get his fingers around the man's neck for the past two years.

As further punishment, he was ordered to spend the day with his FBI handler, filling in the gaps in his final report for Adams. The office was half-empty. Everyone who didn't have an important case running took the day off for Christmas Eve.

"So after I told you to come in and bring Miss Jordan

with you, you set up a meeting with Kenny Briggs, a known member of a domestic terrorist cell, without notifying the FBI?"

"That's correct."

Adams's face grew bleaker and bleaker as the conversation went on, his eyes heavier and heavier with disapproval.

Reid shrugged. "You got Kenny and his brother, right?" Cade had dropped them off without any trouble.

"That's not the point," Adams objected. Then huffed out some air. "So, acting on information you received from Briggs, you single-handedly infiltrated a suspected terrorist location?"

"I had Miss Jordan with me. She's damn good backup."

"Don't remind me." Adams shook his head. Since he was Reid's handler, his behind was on the line, too. "What were you thinking, bringing a civilian into that mess?"

"That she had a right. Nobody had as much at stake as she did." And he hadn't wanted to let her out of his sight. And even if he had, she wouldn't have stayed behind, short of him handcuffing her to the steering wheel. "She's a tough woman. She could handle it."

Adams watched him for a long second, assessing. "Do you have a personal relationship with Miss Jordan?"

"She's the mother of my children."

"Have you had a sexual relationship with Miss Jordan while on this mission?" Adams clarified.

"I don't see how that's your business." The muscles in Reid's jaw were beginning to tighten. He had no idea how to define what had happened between them. Couldn't come to terms with any of that over the past two days. Memories of the time they'd spent together kept surfacing at the most inopportune moments to drive him crazy.

"Do you realize the liability you subjected this agency to?" Adams was about gritting his teeth.

Tension-filled silence stretched between them, Reid trying hard not to just get up and walk out and to hell with procedure. For the colonel's sake, he would sit through this and play along if it killed him.

Adams went back to his notes. "It says here that you took out one man before entering the building. He was talking to Jimmy Briggs."

That was the surprise of the day. Jimmy Sparks was actually Jimmy Briggs, Kenny's second cousin—Kenny had confessed that morning in custody. Jimmy had been using the Sparks name in Hopeville as cover. The relationship explained why Kenny had advanced in the ranks despite his lack of aptitude. This close to the attack, Jimmy, now confirmed as the head of the cell, was relying more and more on family, the only members of his team he really trusted.

"And you didn't see Joey Briggs there?"

Reid shook his head. Joey was Kenny's middle brother. To have him and Jimmy loose somewhere out there left an uneasy feeling in Reid's stomach. "Any idea where they were going to release the virus?"

"According to Kenny, at the Parson Hill courthouse. That's where his father was convicted."

Made sense. Kenny and his brothers' main motivation was to bring down the government. Might as well start their crusade against government at the local level, where they also had a personal score to settle. And now that Reid knew that Jimmy Sparks was Jimmy Briggs, Kenny's cousin, that explained a lot, too. Jimmy's and Kenny's fathers had received the death sentence together. "So Kenny is singing?"

"We used his little brother as leverage." Adams looked away, obviously feeling the hypocrisy since he had, at the beginning of the debriefing, faulted Reid for doing just that.

"What else did he say?"

"There was also supposed to be an assassination attempt at city hall during the mayor's Christmas-morning speech tomorrow. According to Kenny, the guy who was supposed to take the mayor out was shot at the slaughterhouse. Kenny identified everyone from the crime-scene photos. We're sending an undercover SWAT team to city hall anyway and have increased security and all that."

An attempt to assassinate the mayor. The mayor who had been the prosecuting attorney at the trials of the Briggs brothers back in the day. A half-formed thought cast a shadow over Reid. "Out of curiosity, what's the governor doing for the holidays?"

"How should I know?"

"Two decades ago, the Briggs brothers, Kenny's and Jimmy's fathers, got the death penalty at the Parson Hill courthouse. The current mayor was the prosecuting attorney. The current governor was the judge."

Adams went completely still. "Kenny said something about the holy trinity of revenge. We figured it meant Jimmy, Kenny and Billy."

"Except there's Joey Briggs, too. Still out there." Along with Jimmy, able to execute the third prong of their revenge mission, if there was a third prong.

Adams was already on the phone to the governor's security detail. "So the security issues we discussed earlier might not be completely resolved," he started. "Would you read me the governor's schedule for the holidays?" He listened. "I see."

"What is it?" Reid asked when Adams had hung up.

"The governor is doing last-minute Christmas shopping at the North-East Philadelphia Mall as a publicity ploy to boost the economy." He glanced at his watch. "Right about now. Then he's taking off until the New Year."

Reid's mind was churning furiously. That guy outside the slaughterhouse had refused to allow his wife to go to the mall with the kids. "What do we know about Joey Briggs?" he asked, then answered his own question. "Up until a few years ago, he was a normal guy. Worked all kinds of construction jobs, including demolition. Then he got caught up in Kenny's circle."

"Demolition," Adams said, scowling fiercely.

"A three-pronged approach. The virus at the courthouse. The assassination of the mayor. And a bomb at the mall for the governor."

Adams was dialing already.

And Reid was running out the door. One of the last things Lara had told him was that she would be taking the twins to the mall to have their picture taken with Santa today. The North-East Philly Mall was the nearest one to Hopeville.

THE MALL WAS PACKED because of the governor's visit, news cameras positioned everywhere. If Lara had realized the place would be this mobbed, she would have made an effort to get here earlier. She pushed her double stroller past a row of gaily decorated stores on the mall's upper level. The twins were quiet, happy as clams, thanks to their complimentary candy canes.

Their pictures with Santa were carefully tucked into her purse. She'd gotten extras, for Reid and his mother, although she had no idea how to get in touch with either of them. She expected Reid would eventually call to work something out. He hadn't yet. She held the pain of that inside. She wasn't going to mope around. She wasn't going to ruin Christmas for Zak and Nate. If her heart was breaking, nobody had to know about it.

She scanned the store windows, wishing she could have afforded to put more people on her Christmas list. Maybe next year. Her business was growing slowly, but steadily. She had a good reputation. Word was getting around. Maybe before too long the lean years would finally be behind them.

"Easy with the sugar rush." She grinned at her boys, love filling her to the brim. Then she looked up—navigating a twin stroller in the crowd wasn't easy—and…

The only reason she recognized the man was because he was the spitting image of his brothers, Kenny and Billy Briggs. She didn't remember the name Reid had said, but she was certain that the man coming out of the maintenance corridor, looking nervously around, was the third Briggs brother.

A cheer went up downstairs.

She looked over the liberally garlanded railing. The governor making a speech, giving his best syrupy smile to the cameras.

The Briggs brother stopped to watch, hate distorting his face. Then his narrow lips tilted up in an evil smile.

Every instinct she had told her that he wasn't here to do his last-minute Christmas shopping. According to Reid, the group the Briggs were part of was not only antigovernment but antireligion and anticapitalist, too, rejecting all consumerism, which they saw as the rich sucking the blood of the poor. They basically held a grudge against everyone they perceived as ever having done them wrong.

He glanced at his watch, then walked straight toward her, eyeing his watch again, picking up speed. He sure looked like he was anxious to get out of here all of a sudden.

Where was he headed? She looked behind her, her

eyes settling on the fire stairs that led to an emergency exit. The way he scurried forward reminded her of a rat running from a sinking ship.

Which gave her a really, really bad feeling.

She glanced around desperately. Saw a security guard at the top of the escalator. It would take minutes for her to get over there while pushing a double-wide stroller through the crowd of last-minute shoppers. And even if she did get to the guard quickly, would he believe her? She didn't have time to convince him that something terrible was about to happen, although every instinct she had screamed it.

Which meant she had to somehow get everyone out of the mall on her own. She did the only thing she could think of. She picked the twins up out of the stroller and supported one on each hip, then ran for the escalator, yelling, "Fire! Fire! Get out!", causing instant panic.

If she was wrong, she'd be in trouble for raising a false alarm. If she was right, she might just save the life of every man, woman and child in here. "Fire!" she screamed.

Then the Briggs guy was there, smashing his elbow into her temple, taking her down, then dragging her and the twins into that maintenance corridor with him. Nobody paid any attention to them in the stampede.

"MOST EVERYONE WAS evacuated, but Joey Briggs has a couple of hostages, including the governor. By the time we called the governor's security detail it was too late. There was such chaos, his team couldn't get him out.

Briggs is demanding a safe getaway and the release of his brothers from prison or he'll blow up the building," the senior FBI officer on the scene updated Reid. Adams had called ahead and let them know that Reid had valuable knowledge of the possible perpetrators. Apparently, when the governor's life was on the line, past sins were quickly forgiven.

"And we don't think he's acting alone," the FBI officer went on. "When he gave his demands, there was a male voice in the background that seemed to be giving him orders."

"Jimmy Briggs?"

"That would make the most sense."

Reid's burn scars tingled on his chest. He wasn't going to forget Jimmy's face, backlit by the fire in the bakery, as long as he lived. He would have welcomed a face-to-face meeting with the bastard under different circumstances, but at the moment all he could think of was Lara and their babies.

Her car was in the parking lot. He'd tried to call her cell. She didn't pick up. He hoped against hope that Lara and the boys weren't in there, that they had somehow escaped. But he couldn't escape the dark foreboding that was settling on him.

A man in a black SWAT uniform was running toward them. "There's another complication, sir," he reported.

"What is it?" His boss barked the words at him.

"The main gas lines servicing the north side of the city go right under the parking lot. If there's a large enough explosion at the mall, all that propane could catch fire, too."

Had Jimmy Briggs known that, or was it just a happy coincidence? Reid swore under his breath.

"If that gas line goes, it'll take out a number of blocks surrounding the mall. You better start evacuations," Reid told the senior agent. "I'm going in."

"Like hell you are. You're here to provide intelligence only. The governor's life is at stake. There'll be no rogue missions here."

"Try and stop me."

The FBI man took a step forward, signaling to some of the SWAT team that gathered behind him. "I can and I will." But a phone call cut off the rest of what he was about to say. "Yes, sir. Yes, sir," he was saying, then put away his phone, dark thunder looming on his face. He signaled the SWAT team back. "You're cleared to go in."

Thank you, Colonel, Reid thought as he took off running.

THEY WERE IN THE MALL'S security office, the half-dozen attackers watching a wall of monitors, the half-dozen hostages tied to chairs, except for Lara, whose hands were left unbound so she could keep the babies quiet. When all hell had broken lose, every bad guy in the building had grabbed a hostage, Jimmy Briggs going for the prize—the governor. Apparently, they had planned for every contingency.

She looked around at the others who'd been in the

wrong place at the wrong time. Governor Ferriss looked a little worse for wear, his chin scraped. One of his bodyguards was with him and his forehead was bleeding. An older woman was mumbling prayers under her breath, one after the other. Two teenage girls hung on to each other in the corner, silently crying.

"Look, the only way this could end well is if you let us go," the governor's bodyguard was saying, trying to negotiate not for the first time since they'd been brought here.

"My definition of a good ending is you dead and me walking away." Jimmy Briggs smirked at him, then went back to the monitor that showed the parking lot, which was rapidly clearing, except for the police and several SWAT teams. They were removing all civilians from the premises.

"Listen to me, nobody has gotten hurt yet. You could still get off with a minor charge, maybe not even serve time, just probation," the bodyguard lied through his teeth. Jimmy had kidnapped the governor. They weren't going to let him go with a slap on the wrist.

He must have known that because he said, "I ain't goin' back to jail."

The phone rang. He turned his back to the hostages to pick it up, the overhead lights glinting off his bald head.

"I want a helicopter and a million in cash. I want all your men to clear the parking lot. I can see you on the security cameras, so don't try to pull anything," he said to whoever was on the other end.

"I have the whole mall rigged with explosives. You don't do what I say, I blow her up. You have an hour to get what I want." He ended the call without waiting for an answer.

He acted the man in charge, as if everything was exactly as planned, but there was plenty of tension around his eyes. He might have had a plan B in case a standoff like this occurred, but it wasn't his preferred plan. Lara figured the original plan had been to set the bombs, get out, blow up the building with the governor in it.

She'd messed that up. Immediate disaster had been averted. But she wasn't sure if all she'd done was postpone the inevitable.

Lara held Zak and Nate closer, burying her face against their warm little bodies. "We'll be good and quiet for a little while, okay? Then we'll go home. And guess what? Tomorrow morning Santa is coming."

"Sa sa," Nate said, his cinnamon eyes all lit up.

"Santa," she corrected out of habit.

"He he," Zak said.

"No TV here, honey. But when we get home, we'll watch Henry Hero, I promise." She made sure to keep her face averted from the bad guys in the room.

Jimmy hadn't recognized her so far. Of course, they hadn't seen each other much back in Hopeville. Her butcher shop had been open for only two weeks before it had burned. And she looked different now. Gained some weight with the babies. Cut her hair short.

He might also recognize the twins. He'd been in that slaughterhouse where they'd been held. She was counting on the fact that he was a guy, his mind too busy with evil plans to pay much attention to a couple of kids. He'd gone to that slaughterhouse to discuss business. It was entirely possible that he hadn't even glanced at the crib.

What would happen if he did recognize them, the boys or her? She'd been chewing on that for the last twenty minutes. She could tie him to a different identity. Was that important enough to him to kill her straightaway? He meant to kill all of them anyway, what would that matter?

Still, instinct told her to keep her head down and stay as invisible as possible. Extra attention from a deranged terrorist was the last thing she wanted. Not unless they were one-on-one and she had a cleaver handy.

Because she wasn't about to forget that this was the man responsible for kidnapping her babies. This was the man responsible for her shop burning down. This was the man responsible for burning Reid.

"You have the whole mall up on those monitors," the governor's security guard said to Jimmy. "How come we don't see any of your bombs?"

"In the ventilation system."

The bodyguard didn't look convinced. "How did you get into the ventilation system without any of these cameras seeing what you were doing? They have every square inch of the mall covered."

"Not the restrooms. That would be illegal." Jimmy gave a superior grin.

"Do you know how many tons of explosives it would take to do in a building of this size?"

Jimmy finally lost his patience and whirled on the man, pointed his gun at the guy's head. His eyes said, *be quiet or be dead.*

The bodyguard pressed his lips together and leaned back in his chair, exchanging a look with the governor. Lara prayed that they wouldn't underestimate the attackers and try something stupid.

Among the hostages, she was the only one who knew about Jimmy's and his cousin Joey's background. And she was willing to bet a year's supply of filet mignon that they were exactly right about the amount of explosives.

Chapter Thirteen

Reid came in through the roof, straight into the ventilation system, and was met with a helluva surprise. Enough C4 was rigged all over the place to take down the building and then some, almost certainly setting off the explosion of the propane main line. The charges were distributed evenly throughout the vast ventilation ducts, from what he could see so far.

The good news was, he was in the building and had the location of the bombs. The bad news was, although he wasn't a complete novice, he wasn't a bomb specialist. It would have taken him a day to disarm them all, if he was very, very lucky.

And they definitely didn't have a day, or even half of one. Only one hour was allowed by Jimmy Briggs. Out of that hour, Reid had already used fifteen minutes getting into the place unseen.

Didn't look good so far. But he was ready to do anything to get the hostages out, save them or die trying. The odds were pretty long on the *die* part. And there was a chance that Lara and the twins were trapped somewhere below him.

He couldn't stand not knowing how they fared, what they were doing. Walking away from them had sounded great in theory. He hadn't realized until now that it was mission impossible.

He got his cell out and texted, Bombs confirmed, vents, to the team leader waiting outside. He didn't want to risk talking; the vent system would have carried his voice. They had a team of explosives experts as well as a robot, but they couldn't get them onto the roof. It was one thing for a commando secret soldier who was trained in escape and evasion to get in. A whole team with their clumsy protective suits would never make it.

He was alone in this.

For the first time ever, the thought of that didn't make him happy.

Lara and Zak and Nate, not to mention the rest of the hostages, depended on him. The best he could do was start disarming the bombs where he was and keep going, get as much done as possible before time was up. He wouldn't be able to get to them all. He would go down with whatever was left over. But there was a small chance that the hostages were in the part of the building that he would make safe.

He began with grim determination, pulling his tools from a small pocket in his boots. Blue wire or red wire? He followed each from start to destination. The blue, he thought, then clipped, holding his breath, sweat beading on his forehead.

The unit didn't blow.

His shoulders slumped with relief.

He moved on to the next device. On this, the wires were green and yellow, so his experience with the first one didn't mean anything. Once again, he sweated it out, held his breath and succeeded.

Five minutes had passed. He'd disarmed two bombs. There had to be at least a hundred throughout the building. And, at any time, his luck could run out. That he wouldn't set off a single bomb, would get the wires right every single time, was statistically impossible.

The perfect time for swearing his heart out, but he was a father now and just yesterday he had promised himself to let go of that habit. "Fudge cookies," he said instead, with feeling. Then cringed. If his SDDU buddies could hear him now…

His cell phone vibrated in his pocket.

Speaking of the devil.

We're here, the text message from Cade said.

Reid's mouth tightened. Cade was about to be a father himself any day now. He had no business being here. Nobody expected it of him. It wasn't his mission. He didn't have to get hurt. They weren't a team.

Here where? He texted back while moving on to the next bomb.

On the roof.

He looked at the wires, sweat rolling down his forehead. How many?

Me. Carly. Nick. Spike.

At each name, Reid blinked. How on earth had Cade brought a dream team like that together? And why on earth had they come? Each was or had been with the SDDU. Each was legendary. He knew them, sure, but they weren't best friends. Each had kids. Why would they risk everything for him?

I work alone, he texted back, then put the phone down to cut the red wire. Held his breath.

Nothing blew.

He picked up the phone. He had a message waiting. Not anymore.

A strange feeling filled him. All these people showing up. For him. He felt a little choked up, to be truthful. But he didn't have the time to analyze what it meant, how it fit into his lone-wolf rules. He wrote, Vents are filled with C4.

We'll handle that, Cade wrote, go get to hostages.

Reid moved forward, abandoning the guesswork with the wires, looking down every time he came to a grate. Every store he could see was empty. He headed to the north wing where the security offices were. Even if Jimmy Briggs and his men weren't there, a guy must be keeping an eye on the monitors. And that guy could tell him where the rest of them were and what they had in the way of weapons.

He'd gotten a glimpse at the mall's blueprint before he'd sneaked into the building and was navigating now by memory. Ten endless minutes passed before he came to a point where the ducts were so corroded he knew without a doubt that if he put his weight on that section, he would fall right through the ceiling.

Half an hour of Jimmy's ultimatum was gone.

Reid backed up until he hit the nearest restroom. He came out of the vents there, opened the door a fraction of an inch. Pulled the silencer from his pocket and twisted it on. Aimed for the security camera in the ceiling.

All of that took no more than three seconds. There were hundreds of security cameras in the mall. The images they transmitted most likely rotated through the screens at the security office. And whoever was surveilling the monitors couldn't watch them all at the same time. Chances were, they would just notice that one camera was no longer functioning. They wouldn't know what had happened.

"WE GOT A VISITOR," Joey was saying. He froze the image on one of the monitors, a bathroom door opening an inch or two, the barrel of a gun coming out, the image going grainy.

The whole thing lasted seconds, and the gap in the door showed only a sliver of the man's face, a long straight nose, part of his lips. It meant nothing to Joey.

But Lara knew those lips. Her heart slammed against her rib cage.

"Daddy's here," she whispered to her babies.

Jimmy was swearing loudly, sending two of his goons off to find the intruder. Four of them remained. But she and her kids were the only ones untied among the hostages, so overpowering those four men was out of the question. Although...she'd seen the governor's bodyguard straining against his nylon cuffs whenever their captors weren't watching. Maybe if he got free...

For now, she did the best that she could, which was to slowly draw closer to the metal filing cabinet in the corner. It looked heavy enough to take cover behind when all hell broke loose eventually. If Reid was here, he was coming for her and the twins; she had no doubt about that.

He came for us. That had to mean something.

She could almost see him, rushing forward in that half-crouch commando move of his, running into the fight to save whoever was in trouble. To save her and their babies. And then her heart turned over in her chest. No matter what she'd tried to pretend since he'd left her at the hotel, whether he wanted them or not, whether he was the exact opposite of a family man or not, she was still, and probably would be forever, irrevocably in love with him.

Gunfire sounded somewhere outside the office, coming from the direction of the food court. Zak started crying. Nate wiggled down from her lap. She let him, holding on to him with one hand, not wanting him to go anywhere near the bad guys. She had no illusion of them holding back for small children.

She was kissing the top of Zak's head—trying to calm the crying before it annoyed anyone with a gun—when the governor's bodyguard bumped her in the shoulder. She glanced back. The man stared forward, toward Jimmy and his men. Lifted his hands behind his back. His wrists were bloody, but he had somehow gotten free.

More gunshots came from outside. Jimmy sent two

more guys to see what was going on. Only he and Joey were left. It was now or never. She set Zak on the floor, too, pushing both boys toward the filing cabinet, rolling her chair in front of them. Then she exchanged another glance with the bodyguard.

Joey was smaller than Jimmy so she lunged for him, caught him by surprise, brought him down hard as the bodyguard went for Jimmy. Joey's head smacked against the sharp edge of the table—pure luck. She was kneeling on his windpipe when a deafening shot went off behind her.

By the time she whipped around, all she could see was the bodyguard on the floor with a hole in his head, and Jimmy's gun pointed at her. She stood immediately, hands in the air. Jimmy backhanded her with the gun. Her head spun, but she held steady.

Zak and Nate were screaming, running to her. Jimmy shoved them back roughly, then grabbed her by the arm. "Do I know you?" He examined her closely.

The old lady, who'd looked ready to faint the whole time, was now holding the boys with her legs, to keep them from coming back and getting into more trouble. Lara shot the woman a grateful look, shaking her head in response to Jimmy's question. He shoved his gun barrel under her chin and lifted her head. Just as the door crashed open.

Reid stood in the demolished doorway, legs apart, both hands on his weapon, murder in his eyes. It was the most glorious sight she'd ever seen.

Jimmy released a sound of surprise, moving his gun

to Reid, but grabbing Lara's arm to use her as a shield. "How the hell are you alive?"

"Let her go," Reid ordered.

And for a split second it looked like Jimmy was considering it, glancing at the governor, probably thinking that he ought to be holding the most valuable hostage. Then his gaze went from Reid to her and a cold smile stretched his lips. "I'll be damned. I knew I knew her from somewhere. Old lovers reunited. How sweet it is, heh?" He laughed. "Man she was hot that night. You were busy when we came for you, so we let you finish. You were gonna die anyway, why not let you have that last piece of meat. I might not be a saint, but I'm not a complete bastard."

Reid's face went a shade darker.

She about died of embarrassment. Jimmy and his men had watched them make love? Her skin crawled at the thought.

"I always thought I'd come back for her, but things came up." As did Jimmy's hand to cup her breast.

And that was that.

The next second he was blown back, blood squirting from his chest. He could have squeezed off a last shot, but instead he dropped his gun and reached for his pocket.

She dove for her boys, Reid dove for her, putting his strong arms around them. Not a second too soon. An explosion of apocalyptic measures shook the building.

A COUPLE OF MONITORS got shaken off the walls. The ceiling tiles crashed to the floor. But the room remained standing, thanks to Cade and the others. Every bone in Reid's body had been shaken, and when he'd dived for Lara and his boys, he'd landed on his bad hip. The pain was about killing him. So he decided to stay down. The rescue team was on its way. They could handle the rest.

"Reid? Are you all right?" Lara was brushing the dust off his face.

"As long as I got you and Zak and Nate." He wouldn't move his arms from around them. "I'm not going anywhere."

"Good. Stay still until medical rescue gets here." She was checking him over with one hand, checking the kids with the other.

They looked fine to him. They weren't crying anymore, content as long as they had their mother. They were examining him curiously. He must have looked a sight with all the dirt. The ventilation ducts hadn't been kind to him.

"I meant long term. I'd like to stick around."

She tilted her head. "What about the lone-wolf thing?"

"I was wrong. I need people. I need you. All three of you. Thing is, I love you, Lara." That was the God's honest truth, and the best reason he could give her. If that wasn't enough…

But it must have been, because she was kissing him the next second.

He felt the boys tugging at her from behind.

"Santa Claus?" Nate was asking pretty clearly for his first official words.

"Henry Hero," Zak said.

Lara was laughing and crying at the same time as she pulled away and gathered the boys between them. "Even better, guys. This is your daddy."

They blinked solemnly. Then flashed the sweetest baby grins he'd ever seen, and his heart melted.

"Mine," he said as he put his arms around all three, the word coming from the most primal part of him.

"Forever," Lara promised.

Epilogue

"I'm closing." Lara stopped in the doorway that connected the two shops, glancing outside through the window to her right, watching the falling snow for a second. She was ready to go home to the kids.

It'd been a busy day. Business was booming. The twins had become the mascots for the two stores, running from one to the other all day, the babysitter—or Grandma when she was visiting, which was often—gamely following. They were only taken away for walks in the park and taken home for a few hours each afternoon for a nap. Of course, in a few months that schedule would change. They were almost four. They'd be starting preschool soon.

Reid wiped his hands on a cloth, then came closer, took her lips in a searing kiss. "I'll go home with you for a while. The bread needs time to rise."

Something between them clearly didn't.

He nudged her against the wall and deepened the kiss, exploring her mouth with his clever tongue, caressing her breasts with his knowing hands. He was incorrigible.

"Slow day?"

"All the villains of the world must be taking time off for the holidays. I sent the guys home," he told her.

Which meant they were alone. Heat shot through her as he dragged the pad of his thumbs across her nipples. He moved the kissing lower, seducing her neck, lingering in the hollow spot, moving agonizingly slowly toward those hardening buds. Then his mouth found one, which freed up a hand. He used that to reach under her knee and hook it over his hip, pressing the proof of his desire against her.

"We should visit our old friend the dough-kneading table," he said in a heated whisper.

"The last time you said that, you got me pregnant. Again." She rolled her eyes, her gaze straying up. The next second she was moving away from him. "The cameras!" When he touched her, she had a tendency to forget about everything else.

He came after her, not looking the least perturbed. His gaze focused on the spot where her shirt gaped. "I'll delete the tape before anyone comes into work in the morning." He splayed his fingers across her belly. She was only three months along, barely showing. "I'm glad I'm here with you for this pregnancy," he told her, his voice full of tenderness. "I didn't realize until now what I missed with the twins. It really is a miracle. Cade wasn't messing with me."

He kissed her hotly and deeply, just as a faint alarm beeped in the back office. He tore himself away as if it pained him.

She straightened her clothes. Ben and the others would be here any minute. They would receive the alarm on their cells.

Due to the economy, a lot of stores had gone out of business in the small strip mall. And every time one did, the top-secret unit Reid worked for bought the place. They put a man behind the counter as a front. Business continued as usual. But in the sizable attic that stretched above the row of stores, a super high-tech mission center had been sneakily built.

Reid had found a way to do his job and still keep them safe. The strip mall's security—although invisible to the untrained eye—rivaled that of the White House. And since Reid was the coordinator, he rarely left on missions; he arranged for background support when needed, utilizing his considerable knowledge of the field.

Oddly, business also began doing better than ever before. The strip mall was gaining steadily in popularity, especially with the ladies. The men on Reid's team, handsome hunks to the last, didn't escape notice.

"I suppose I won't be home early tonight," he said grumpily.

"I suppose not. You're the mission coordinator."

He raised a dark eyebrow. "I prefer spymaster."

She grinned.

"I will not be mocked." He kissed her thoroughly.

"Lesson learned," she said when she could breathe again.

His gaze searched her face. "I'm sorry. I had plans for us for tonight. You don't mind?"

"I knew who you were when I married you. I love you with everything that you do, exactly the way you are."

"I love you, too. You and the boys are the best thing that has ever happened to me." The reluctance was still there in his eyes, but his stance was already changing, his body language morphing into warrior mode.

Cars pulled into the parking lot. The team was here. He kissed her one more time then took off running.

She said a prayer for whoever was in trouble this time. Then she turned to go home to her boys, who'd be awaiting their mother's embrace.

Maybe she didn't end up a brave pilot like Granny Jordan, but she was raising twin boys, and that was an adventure and a half. And nobody could argue that the man she married wasn't plenty exciting. No, she wasn't living her grandmother's life. But she wasn't living her mother's, either. And that was as it should be.

She had her own life, her own challenges, her own wonderful family. Her very own spymaster who was about to save Christmas. Again.

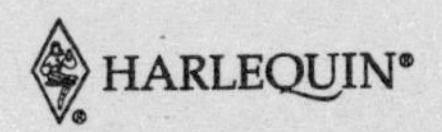

INTRIGUE®

COMING NEXT MONTH

Available November 9, 2010

#1239 BODY ARMOR
Bodyguard of the Month
Alana Matthews

#1240 HIGH-CALIBER CHRISTMAS
Whitehorse, Montana: Winchester Ranch Reloaded
B.J. Daniels

#1241 COLBY BRASS
Colby Agency: Christmas Miracles
Debra Webb

#1242 SAVIOR IN THE SADDLE
Texas Maternity: Labor and Delivery
Delores Fossen

#1243 THE PEDIATRICIAN'S PERSONAL PROTECTOR
The Delancey Dynasty
Mallory Kane

#1244 HOSTAGE TO THUNDER HORSE
Elle James

HICNM1010

See below for a sneak peek from
our inspirational line, Love Inspired® Suspense

Enjoy this heart-stopping excerpt from
RUNNING BLIND
by top author Shirlee McCoy,
available November 2010!

The mission trip to Mexico was supposed to be an adventure. But the thrill turns sour when Jenna Dougherty and her roommate Magdalena are kidnapped.

"It's okay. I'm here to help." The voice was as deep as the darkness, but Jenna Dougherty didn't believe the lie. She could do nothing but lie still as hands slid down her arms, felt the rope around her wrists.

"I'm going to use a knife to cut you free, Jenna. Hold still."

The cold blade of a knife pressed close to her head before her gag fell away.

"I—" she started, but her mouth was dry, and she could do nothing but suck in air.

"Shhh. Whatever needs to be said can be said when we're out of here." Nick spoke quietly, his hand gentle on her cheek. There and gone as he sliced through the ropes on her wrists and ankles.

He pulled her upright. "Come on. We may be on borrowed time."

"I can't leave my friend," Jenna rasped out.

"There's no one here. Just us."

"She has to be here." Jenna took a step away.

"There's no one here. Let's go before that changes."

"It's dark. Maybe if we find a light…"

"What did you say?"

"We need to turn on the light. I can't leave until I know that—"

"What can you see, Jenna?"

"Nothing."

"No shadows? No light?"

"No."

"It's broad daylight. There's light spilling in from the window I climbed in through. You can't see it?"

She went cold at his words.

"I can't see anything."

"You've got a nasty bruise on your forehead. Maybe that has something to do with it." His fingers traced the tender flesh on her forehead.

"It doesn't matter *how* it happened. I'm blind!"

Can Nick help Jenna find her friend or will chasing this trail have Jenna running blindly again into danger?

Find out in RUNNING BLIND, available in November 2010 only from Love Inspired Suspense.

SHLISEXP1110